COCAINE

COCAINE

Massimo Carlotto
Gianrico Carofiglio
Giancarlo De Cataldo

Translated from the Italian by
Shaun Whiteside, Howard Curtis and Alan Thawley

MACLEHOSE PRESS
QUERCUS · LONDON

First published in the Italian language as *Cocaina* by
Giulio Einaudi editore s.p.a., Turin, in 2013
First published in Great Britain in 2015 by

MacLehose Press
An imprint of Quercus Publishing Ltd
Carmelite House
50 Victoria Embankment
London EC4Y 0DZ

An Hachette UK company

Campagna's Trail © 2012, Massimo Carlotto
The Speed of the Angel © 2012, Gianrico Carofiglio
The White Powder Dance © 2012, Giancarlo de Cataldo
© 2013 Giulio Einaudi editore s.p.a., Turin

English translations copyright © 2015 by Shaun Whiteside,
© 2015 by Howard Curtis and © 2015 by Alan Thawley
Copy-edited by Andrea P. A. Belloli

A CIP catalogue record for this book is available
from the British Library.

ISBN (HB) 978 0 85705 330 5
ISBN (Ebook) 978 1 84866 597 2

10 9 8 7 6 5 4 3 2 1

Designed and typeset in Bembo by Jouve (UK), Milton Keynes
Printed and bound in Great Britain by Clays Ltd, St Ives plc

CONTENTS

Campagna's Trail

MASSIMO CARLOTTO

Translated by Shaun Whiteside

ISPETTORE GIULIO CAMPAGNA WALKED OVER TO THE members of the flying squad. Two officers from his unit were keeping an eye on the onlookers crowding around, trying to work out why on earth the cops had broken into that flat in Padua's old ghetto during happy hour. Most of the crowd were students, young professionals and shop assistants sipping spritzers from big plastic tumblers. A moment before they had filled the surrounding bars, but the rumour had spread quickly. Ispettore Campagna had himself been having a drink with a few friends in a square not far away when he had got a call from Damiano Pinamonti, his colleague in charge of the operation.

"Giulio, we've only found 300 grams."

"Have another look. My informer was absolutely certain."

"Help me out here," Pinamonti whispered. "Please."

Campagna snorted and muttered a curse. Then he gulped down what remained of his wine and left the bar, followed by the jokes of his friends. The Paduans were masters in the art of taking the piss. The inspector didn't need to be present during the search, and his arrival would make it clear that he had been the one who had served up the tip on a silver platter. That wasn't good, because it could lead to people identifying his source. The thing that made Campagna force his way through the rubberneckers was that Pinamonti was racking up failures one after the other, and at this rate he would end up buried in an office somewhere. In fact, he was just a good policeman going through a bad patch. Everybody went through periods like this. The only difference was how long they lasted. In his colleague's case, it was becoming an embarrassment.

One of the officers looked away from a girl's cleavage.

"You're always on duty, Campagna."

"That way I'll get my career over with quicker," he replied, tossing his cigarette butt away.

The two policemen laughed heartily. Campagna had stopped caring about his career some time ago; he'd been in the force for so long that they would never fire him. On more than one occasion the head of the flying squad had had to advocate hard on his behalf. The inspector was prone to getting into trouble because he didn't care about rules and hierarchies. But he was a good and honest man. And he didn't let go until he had closed a case. The consensus was that he was eccentric, a bit crazy. That assessment happened to coincide with Campagna's view of himself.

Winking at the officer guarding the door, he climbed the stairs, quickening his pace as he went.

The flat had been recently done up. It smelled of paint and floor wax, but the few pieces of furniture were in poor taste. Clearly no-one lived there. It was a base of operations for sales in the city centre, where the dealers took orders and picked up the quantities requested. There would have been constant coming and going. All Campagna's informer had to do was follow them a few times to figure how the business worked. Campagna looked round, assessing things quickly as he always did. He stepped into the big, untidy sitting room. Two guys were seated on the only sofa with their hands cuffed behind their backs. Very tightly, judging by the expressions on their faces. The two dealers gave him an apparently cursory glance, but in their minds Campagna had been filed under the heading of "cop".

"Here you are at last," his colleague said nervously. He showed the inspector a clear plastic bag containing at least 300 grams of heroin. "These two bastards aren't talking."

"Who are they?" the inspector asked. In fact he knew very well who they were, but he wanted to go on playing the role of the *ingénue* to the very end.

The other inspector played along. "These two Tunisians have been going in and out of this flat," he said. He walked over to the men and gave one of them a slap. "But they're refusing to tell us where the rest of the stuff is."

"There isn't any more," the other man stammered, immediately receiving a kick to the shins.

"Stop being a dick," Pinamonti shouted.

Campagna took a look around the flat. In the course of the police search, the furniture and kitchen appliances had been smashed into tiny pieces. There was no sign of drugs, which meant that they must have been kept in some special hiding-place that had been created while the flat was being refurbished.

Taking Pinamonti aside, Campagna told him of his suspicions.

"I can't take a pickaxe to the place," Pinamonti said.

"Who's the owner?"

"A girl. Milvia Tiso. She bought it and was having it refurbished so that she could rent it out. Eighteen hundred a month."

"What do we know about her?"

"She has no record."

"Married? Children?"

"A husband."

"Have you checked him out?"

Pinamonti ran his hand over his head.

"Fuck, I didn't think of that! Bugger, I can't get anything right!"

Campagna gripped his arm tightly.

"Enough with the performance anxiety, Damiano. We'll sort it."

Taking out his mobile, Campagna called the station. After a few minutes he rang off.

'The owner's husband is Tunisian, and he was born in the same village as one of those two bastards on the sofa."

Pinamonti walked over to the sofa.

"Which one of you is Abdessalem?"

The one on the left nodded.

"That's me."

"We're going to get Dawoud, the guy from your village," Campagna announced. "We're going to have a competition to see which of you is smarter. The first one to talk gets a lighter sentence."

It was the other man who won.

"By the front door, the wall on the right," he said in a strong French accent. "I'm just a street dealer. It was the others who brought the gear."

His mate stared at him in horror before deluging him with insults. The policemen had to hold them apart to keep them from headbutting each other.

The skirting board concealed a gap at least three metres long, containing a series of plastic tubes with screw caps on either end.

"Here we are!" Pinamonti exclaimed with relief. "It must be at least five kilos."

"Six," Campagna corrected him, clapping him on the

shoulder. "Well done. Now organise a nice press conference for the boss and score yourself a few points."

Pinamonti tried to find words to thank him, but Campagna was already on his way out. Passing among the onlookers, he went back to the bar to drink a few more glasses of wine.

Then he walked home to join his wife and daughter. Putting his gun and badge in a drawer, he pretended that he had left his work at the door of the flat. Giulio Campagna was not a tormented soul, or even a particularly worried one. He tried to maintain his dignity in a myriad of complicated situations, without kidding himself that things were ever going to get better. His family was one of those things. He really loved Gaia and Ilaria, the women in his life, but sometimes they were one massive ball-breaker that he had to escape from. He drank and cheated on his wife in the same way that he approached his work: in moderation. And without making too much of a fuss. He just got on with it.

That evening, after a dinner during which he enjoyed listening to his sixteen-year-old daughter's stories about how she had survived a school trip to Venice, Campagna plonked himself down in front of the T.V. with Gaia, resolving to leave work crap behind and allow himself a good night's sleep.

Instead his mobile started ringing. The ringtone was the one reserved for his colleagues. His wife did not move a muscle; she knew what it meant to be married to an officer in the drugs squad. But Campagna looked at his mobile for a long time before answering.

"That Iranian guy's here," area officer Annina Montisci said. "He's just come into the Chinese restaurant on the industrial estate."

"Are you sure?"

"Yes. Get a move on."

Campagna changed back into his uniform and twenty minutes later drove through the gates of a car park. Montisci appeared out of the darkness. She could have been one of a thousand students at the University of Padua. No-one would have guessed that she was a cop, not with that hairdo and those wire-rimmed glasses. In fact she was clever and ambitious. Unlike the inspector she would rise through the ranks. Campagna liked teasing her.

"Have you told your colleagues?" he asked.

"Are you joking? This one is ours."

Campagna laughed and gave her a hug.

"I like you best, Annina." She wriggled away from him.

"Not least because I'm the only one who's willing to work with you."

"What's our friend doing?"

"Eating. Have you had dinner?"

"Yes. You?"

"No."

"Then I'll keep you company. That way we can see if the Iranian meets up with anyone."

The restaurant was huge and full of people. It resembled a self-service restaurant in a South American city: the fixed price menu was reasonable, and you could fill your plate whenever you wanted to. Given the financial crisis, the place was doing good business, and the quality wasn't appallingly poor. Montisci was hungry and took full advantage; Campagna had a beer. They found a table not far from the Iranian, who had already reached the pudding course. He seemed calm. Every now and again he would look around discreetly. He seemed to feel safe, and Campagna could not work out why, given that he was wanted for international drug trafficking and had dodged an eight-year sentence. He wasn't a big shot, he was a repeat offender, and that was all he would ever be. The inspector had seen lots like him. As far as they were concerned, jail was a traffic accident, and once they had served their sentence they would start all over again.

"Are we going to take him out?" Montisci said.

Campagna jerked his head towards a family group sitting nearby.

"Do you want to scare the children?"

The policewoman shrugged.

"He's a quiet type, our Mohammadreza; he'd let us take him away without too much of a fuss."

Campagna hid behind his menu.

"Look who's just arrived."

"Of all the people ..."

Thirty years old, tall, skinny, long hair, a bit tired-looking, he seemed like the kind of person who takes life as it comes and who would not turn his nose up at some gear if it came his way. In fact, Giacomo Floriani was a Chief Superintendent. And a good one, too. He was seldom seen at the station because he spent most of his time in the dodgiest parts of the city trying to catch drug dealers.

"Let's go," Campagna said.

"There goes our arrest," Montisci muttered, disappointed. "And there goes my evening, too. A bit of departmental co-ordination wouldn't go amiss."

Campagna walked towards the till, followed by Montisci. Their colleague had not deigned to look at them, and now he was sitting at the jail-dodger's table, chatting away.

They waited for him in Montisci's car, smoking with the windows open. Spring was on its way and the nights were getting milder. The door of the restaurant opened and the light from the neon sign lit up Floriani's face. Montisci got out of the car.

"You're here for the Iranian, aren't you?" Floriani said, slipping into the back seat.

"Exactly," Campagna said.

"He's all yours. I'm not interested anymore. He's trying to sell a batch of opium."

"Opium?" exclaimed Montisci. "That's a bit niche, and I'm not sure there's much of a market for it in Padua."

"Mohammadreza is on the run and needs some cash," Campagna said. "If he's been reduced to selling unfashionable stuff like that, it means that he's not as important as he once was."

"That's what I think, too," Floriani said, opening the car door. "Once he's gone down, people will stop trusting him. If we put him in the slammer, we'll be doing him a favour."

"Don't you want to be involved?" Montisci said.

"I couldn't give a stuff. He's a second-rater," Floriani replied contemptuously, before disappearing into the darkness.

"What does that make us? Refuse collectors?" Montisci commented acidly.

Campagna did not reply but sat in silence, thinking about his colleague's attitude until they saw the Iranian leave and walk towards a bicycle, the favoured mode of transport of Padua's drug dealers. The trafficker bent over to undo the lock on the chain; a moment later the police were standing behind him.

"You're under arrest, Mohammedreza," Campagna said.

The man did not even bother to show them his fake passport, which had, among other things, cost him a lot of money, and allowed himself to be cuffed without putting up the slightest resistance.

While searching him, Montisci discovered a small brick in the inside pocket of his velvet jacket. She sniffed it.

"Opium?"

The man nodded.

"Mixed with hashish it's a genuine delight for mind and spirit, beautiful lady," he said solemnly.

"You hear that, Giulio?" she exploded with amusement.

"Our friend is a gallant philosopher," Campagna said sarcastically. "That 'delight' of his is going to bring him at least three years on holiday at state expense."

"He might play ball," Montisci murmured. "In which case the sentence will shrink as if by magic."

The Iranian smiled resignedly.

"Forgive me, ladies and gentlemen, but I have a reputation to defend."

Campagna took his arm.

"I know. That's why I'm not going to waste time questioning you. The magistrate can take care of that. I'll take you to the station, and then I'm going home. You aren't. You're going to jail, solitary confinement, to a nice cell that hasn't seen a mop and bucket for a few years.'

The next morning Campagna turned up at his office a good hour late. He was taking things easy.

"Did your alarm not go off?" Pinamonti said in a loud voice, pretending to be serious.

"A meeting with an informer," Campagna said.

"That's true, you mentioned it yesterday," Pinamonti lied.

"I forgot. But the boss has been looking for you since he got in."

For five minutes, then.

"Any idea what he wants?"

"Yes, and you're not going to like it."

"Should I be worried?"

"I don't know. I think it's a routine administrative fuck-up."

"What are you on about, Damiano?" Campagna said, and went and knocked on the door of the "*Dottore*", as everyone called him.

The head of the flying squad was young and elegant and knew his job. He had not got where he was by licking anybody's boots, or because he had the usual powerful people covering for him. Giorgio Lopez was better than the others. He was also skilled at extracting himself diplomatically from the most delicate situations, but never at the cost of his subordinates.

He tapped his index finger on the front page of *Il Mattino di Padova*.

"Read this, Campagna."

The inspector turned the paper around and peered at the headline: "Padua Capital of Cocaine Consumption in the Veneto".

"It's no secret that everybody's snorting, dealing, lining their pockets and investing thanks to cocaine," Campagna said, slightly perplexed. "Only the politicians, when they're not cheerfully consuming the stuff, pretend not to know that the battle's been lost."

"So what are we supposed to do? Forget about it?" Pinamonti said, immediately regretting having broached the subject with Campagna of all people.

"We can only contain the problem by standing up to the gangs, because there are too many consumers," the inspector replied in a tone that was both argumentative and sarcastic. "The real problem is heroin. If things go on like this, we'll find ourselves with yet another army of addicts. Padua was once pretty tough, I can assure you. Some parts of town were practically paved with syringes."

"You don't need to tell me; I used to work in Milan," Lopez snapped. "And don't you come here acting the sociologist, O.K.? Once you put on a uniform, there are some things you can't even think."

Campagna opened his arms wide.

"Sorry! Until a moment ago I thought I was on Planet Earth."

"Don't cross the line, Giulio," Lopez warned him. "Several of your colleagues have complained about your methods. How long has it been since you last arrested anyone, not for dealing but for possession of cannabis?"

"Personal use is gradually being liberalised everywhere," the inspector said in self-defence. "It'll happen here too. There's no point ruining people's lives just because they roll the odd joint."

Lopez sighed. "You have no idea how lucky you are," he murmured. "Your superiors have always covered your back. That's the only reason you're still on the force."

Campagna relaxed. "The truth is that I'm a good boy," he ventured, half-smiling. "Why don't they put me back on Robberies?"

Ignoring the remark, his boss picked up a file and handed it to him.

"You're on cocaine full-time, starting now."

Opening the file, the inspector found himself staring at an all-too-familiar face. He turned pale and gulped. Roberto Pizzo, known as Roby. Campagna, though, had called him Pizzo since childhood, when they had played football in the street on the outskirts of Padua. They had remained friends over the years. The problem was that Pizzo dealt cocaine, and Campagna had protected him on several occasions.

Campagna closed the file.

"Keep me off this case, chief."

"I can't," Pinamonti said irritably. "We're ready to arrest your friend and his gang of losers, but there might be a chance for you to limit the damage you've already done to your career."

"How?"

Lopez opened the file and found another photograph, which he shoved under Campagna's nose.

"Do you know this guy?"

"Never seen him before."

"His name's Tinko Boyev. He's a Bulgarian mafioso, and he's set up a business dealing in coke, 2,000 kilos per cargo, right here in Padua."

The inspector was beginning to see the light.

"You're interested in the Bulgarian, obviously, not in small fry like Pizzo."

"I'm interested in cleaning up the organisation so that we can 'contain the phenomenon', as you might put it. Your friend might be useful, and people who are useful do you favours, and favours need to be repaid. It might be worth their while remaining at liberty until they mess up again."

"I understand."

"I hope so, Giulio. Because this applies to you, too. The days when you could do whatever the hell you liked are over. According to this file you've been protecting a gang of drug traffickers."

"If you put it like that, it doesn't sound so great, but the reality's different. And you know that or you'd have fired me a long time ago."

"According to this file, your goose is cooked," Lopez said. "I'm giving you the chance to put things straight, so long as you don't blow the whole thing sky high."

"Who's going to be in charge of the squad? Pinamonti?"

"There is no squad. You're on your own this time."

Campagna stared at Lopez for a moment and then took back the file.

"I bet when I read this I'll find out the real reason why I'm on my own."

The boss shook his head.

"You're wrong there, too. I'm not telling you anything official. Commissario Pinamonti is under the impression that you've been looking for new leads and that you found this file at random, because no-one in the flying squad ever puts files back in the right place after consulting them."

"You're right, the place is a complete tip," the inspector said.

The phone rang and Lopez waved him away.

Campagna hurried to his desk. He couldn't wait to read the file. An hour later he knew everything. An informer in Pizzo's gang had his balls in the grip of Sovrintendente Capo Floriani. That explained Floriani's rude and arrogant behaviour the previous evening: he was convinced that he was dealing with a bent cop. To an extent this was down to Pizzo, who had boasted clumsily and irresponsibly about having a policeman covering his back. The rumour had done the rounds, getting bigger as it went, until Campagna had found himself being described as Pizzo's accomplice who was pocketing his share at the end of each month.

The situation wasn't disastrous from the legal point of

view, but it was from a disciplinary one. Once the informer had made his deposition in front of a judge, Campagna's career would be finished. Lopez was right: the whole affair needed sorting out. Not least because Campagna was only guilty of considering Pizzo's gang to be unworthy of investigation, on the simple grounds that not only were they a fifth wheel in the gang world but they also performed a useful service to society. The inspector would but have been less than willing to explain this notion to Lopez and his colleagues, but it was one he was absolutely certain about, or had been before opening the file.

But Campagna had been a cop for too long not to understand that there was something else going on now. All that secrecy was over the top, even for a Bulgarian Mafia boss like Tinko Boyev.

He knocked on Lopez's door; his boss smiled ambiguously.

"Doesn't add up, does it?"

Campagna shook his head.

"I can't understand why we're going to such lengths over a gang of mafiosi. Don't tell me it's just to save my career."

Dr Lopez opened a drawer in his desk and took out a photograph of a forty-year-old man in uniform. He handed it to Campagna.

"His name was Marcello Mantovani," Lopez said. "We trained together. He was a great guy, has two small children."

"Did the Bulgarians kill him?"

"Boyev, in person. I know because I was given a tip-off that I can't use as evidence. But I'm sure, absolutely sure, that he was the one who pulled the trigger."

"And now he's going to pay the price, whatever it takes."

"You look like you've got it."

"Perfectly."

"In that case you don't even need to give me regular updates."

Campagna nodded but remained seated, staring at his boss.

"What is it?" Lopez said.

"I've done nothing wrong," Campagna said. "Since cocaine's become all the rage, the floodgates have opened, and an army of people with no criminal records have joined the criminal gangs. These days a cop has to choose between who needs punishing and who doesn't either because he's less dangerous or because he's become a valuable informer."

"You don't need to justify yourself, Giulio," Lopez said. "I know very well that the cocaine trade's a sticky business; it gets your hands dirty. And we're flying without radar because all the rules have gone out the window. Your mistake was to protect Pizzo's gang on a whim, with no apparent advantage to the police service of which you're a member."

"'Even you said the gang were a bunch of losers."

"But if the losers in question aren't useful to me and go on committing crimes, it's my duty to throw him in jail. You're making a mistake, Giulio. Try to understand that."

The inspector got to his feet. He was confused, humiliated. He left the room, forgetting to say goodbye to Lopez. Returning to his desk, he collected his things, slipped the file under his arm and went in search of Pinamonti, who was questioning a Moroccan who had been picked up with 50 grams of coke. Many of the local Mafia gangs used North Africans as street dealers.

"I haven't seen you around here. Who the fuck are you working for?" Pinamonti was asking the man, who was hand-cuffed to a chair.

The Moroccan rattled off a list of names as vague as they were fake. Telling him to go to hell, Pinamonti turned to the inspector.

"How did it go with the chief?"

"Fine. I'm starting today," Campagna said quickly, avoiding his colleague's eye.

"Don't do anything stupid, Giulio. And don't imagine that you can disappear on us. We're short-staffed enough as it is."

Getting into his car, the inspector headed for the Euganean Hills, where he stopped at a trattoria to have a plate of pasta and a steak. He also enjoyed half a litre of house red and washed out his coffee cup with grappa, as he had seen his father and grandfather do. A family tradition that might end with him, given that his daughter did not drink.

Driving back into town, he went to a multiplex where he

chose a film at random. He dozed for a while and then racked his brain for the least painful and illegal way of keeping everybody happy and saving his pension at the same time. He could not come up with a plan. If he wanted to take the Bulgarians' racket apart, avenge his murdered colleague and go on being a cop, everyone else would have to be seen as expendable. He thought again of Lopez's words. The chief was right. He would have to approach the case in a completely different way.

He drove home at dinnertime and pretended nothing was wrong. He went to bed early because Pizzo was a dealer with a very particular clientele. This meant that he had to start work at dawn.

Campagna left the flat just before 5.00 a.m. and joined the queue of traffic travelling along the ring road, heading towards the industrial estate. There were not as many cars as there had once been. The economic crisis had dealt a heavy blow to an area from which lots of companies, sensing hard times ahead, had wisely moved their operations to Romania, Moldavia and China.

He hit a few cafés before he found Pizzo. The dealer was sitting at a table receiving his customers, who first stopped at the counter for a cappuccino and a croissant. Campagna watched him exchanging small talk with some women in blue blouses bearing the logo of a cleaning company. They had been emptying bins and cleaning floors all night, and were returning home to make breakfast for their husbands and children: a line of coke was just what they needed to keep them going.

Then a few men in overalls queued up for their doses. Very small amounts because that was all they could afford. Pizzo's long white hair was gathered up in a ponytail, which made him look like a hippy long past his sell-by-date. But everyone knew and loved him because he too had been a manual labourer, as well as a trade unionist. One of the hard-line ones. Then the company had brought night workers in from across the border from one day to the next and fired everyone else via text message. Pizzo had decided he was done with living a shitty life enriching shitty capitalists, and after working in various bars he had taken up dealing drugs. But he had stayed in the area. Never leaving the industrial estate, he also did not try to expand his racket and invade other people's territory. He had no intention of coming into conflict with the organisations that did the deals that mattered. He sold to a safe and respectable clientele. No-one who snorted his coke would have dreamed of taking to crime. His customers took drugs illegally but for "therapeutic" reasons, in order to survive, the same way Bolivian *campesinos* or miners chewed coca leaves. That was why Campagna had always turned a blind eye to his old friend's activities. It did not strike him as a terrible crime for people whose lives were hard and whose futures were perennially uncertain to seek comfort in "chemicals" paid for with hard-earned cash.

In the end, you could also have said that Pizzo's gang was actually supporting law and order in that they were not feeding the drugs trade by buying drugs. They stole them from other gangs, especially foreign ones. And that advice had come from Campagna himself: "Once you start buying for resale, you'll become competitors, and sooner or later they'll hand you over to the cops. You're better off just taking the stuff."

"And how do we do that?" Roby had asked. "We don't want to go to war with anybody."

"Choose a small gang, but one with a decent-sized racket. Spy on them for a bit, and, once you've identified their courier, nick their gear the first chance you get. But make sure no-one gets hurt, O.K.?"

And that was exactly what they had done, chiefly at the expense of the Albanians and the North Africans.

Pizzo got up and walked towards the door, beckoning to Campagna to follow him. The inspector got into his friend's car, an old Punto. To show up in an expensive car would have been offensive and inappropriate.

"Getting up at dawn every morning takes some of the glamour out of your job as a dealer."

Roby laughed.

"Now I have to go and supply the day labourers. Tell me, what brings you to the wastelands that were once the beating heart of the Veneto's textile industry?"

"You're talking like a trade unionist again."

"The passion still burns within me," Pizzo lied shame-lessly.

"There's a spy inside your gang," the inspector said.

"I know. It's Tony Ceccato," Pizzo said sadly. "He got caught, and he spilled most of the beans to stay out of the nick."

"I'm pleased to see that you've taken it so well," the police-man said. "Tony's packing his things for a fifteen-year trip on the jail circuit."

Pizzo switched gear.

"What do you want me to do? Kill him?" he exploded. "He's done it now. Tony was always a weakling. They took advantage of him at the factory, too."

"At least you've talked to him, haven't you?"

"Of course! He came to me in tears. He apologised and said he'd retract his statement."

"Fat lot of use that's going to be."

"'I know."

Campagna lost patience.

"Fuck it, Pizzo! Won't you give me a straight answer?"

"We're packing our bags," Pizzo said, deciding to tell all. "Betta, me, Gigio and Samuele. We're going to do one last job, then we're going to move abroad to a country with no extradition treaty. I guess there must still be a few?"

"Another gang of Italian hoodlums going to their doom?"

"No, Giulio. We're not as naïve as that. We'll open a piz-zeria, a bar, something like that."

They had no intention whatsoever of working. Pizzo was lying, but the cop continued to play along.

"If you want to open a business, you're going to need a nest-egg."

"We're organising a big sting on a Mafia gang," Pizzo said with a swagger in his voice, "but I can't tell you about it or you'll remember you're a cop and fuck it up for me."

"This time it's going to be different. Tinko Boyev's involved."

When Pizzo heard the name of the Bulgarian Mafia boss, he gripped the steering wheel tightly. His knuckles turned white as marble. Tony Ceccato had fucked up the whole plan.

"Don't take this chance away from me, Giulio. It's the last one I've got. Betta and I are nearly fifty. We're too old to end up in jail."

And I'm too old to lose my pension, Campagna thought.

They drove into a little square faintly lit by the morning sun. Groups of men were chatting and smoking, day labourers for the construction industry. They were waiting for the foremen to come and choose them and drive them to nearby building sites.

Pizzo parked in a corner and a queue formed straightaway. His best customers were bricklayers, roofers, plumbers and electricians. The work was hard, with the tight rhythms of piecework. Coke was the ideal pick-me-up.

Campagna studied the men's faces, marked by exhaustion

and an awareness that nothing in their lives was ever going to change. It was true that everyone snorted coke, rich and poor, graduates and illiterates alike. It was their expectations that made the difference. The Paduan lawyer who had been arrested with his friends a month before had barely raised an eyebrow. The papers had written about it for days because posh Padua always made news. But the people involved protected each other, formed a network, and nothing would happen because there were clearly defined interests to be defended. Coke served to kill boredom, a mild transgression in the smart drawing rooms now frequented by North African dealers.

But those poor wretches who broke their backs climbing up scaffolding, being paid by the hour or the square metre, occupied another planet where getting up at 4.00 a.m. every morning was reason enough to snort a bit of Pizzo's coke, which had been cut many times over anyway.

Looking at them, Campagna felt privileged. He should really have taken out his badge, arrested his friend and identified the customers to report them to the relevant authorities. But he would sooner have shot himself in the balls. He had never been that kind of idiot.

Pizzo spoke quietly and always smiled as he pocketed the money and distributed the bags of coke. He looked like the medicine man of some strange tribe. The vans arrived and everyone ran to stand in line for selection by the foremen. Pizzo and Campagna got back into the Punto.

Roby took a wrap of coke from his pocket.

"The first of the morning is always the best. Want some?" he asked, rolling a five-euro note.

"No, thanks," the policeman said. "I prefer wine, a healthy local product."

"You don't know what you're missing," Pizzo said, lining up the powder on the screen of his iPhone with a supermarket club card. "Coke, if you don't overdo it, is like a religion; it blesses your life. It gives you the answers you need, you know."

"Really?"

"You can depend on it. But if adversity and bad luck have got hold of you, then heroin's your man. The problem is that it kills you if you inject it. But if you snort it, you can save your health. For a few years, obviously."

"It's back in fashion thanks to the Taliban and the Kosovan Mafia."

"The workers will discover it soon enough. Coke in the morning, a syringe of heroin at the end of a shift, and finally nothing but hits of heroin.'

Sighing, Campagna ran his hand over his face.

"Let's go. This place is depressing me."

"I'll take you back to your car, Giulio. I've got to meet my guys shortly. By this time of the day we've seen all our customers."

"You're talking like a sales rep."

Pizzo smiled.

"In a way, that's what I am."

Campagna's tone changed. As cold and hard as if he were throwing a stone in his friend's face.

"No, you're just a piece of shit."

The dealer misinterpreted the change of register.

"This job's making you nervous, Giulio," he said in a conciliatory voice. "You should take a course of dope therapy. Good stuff, obviously. I'll get you some, if you like."

The cop elbowed him in the nose.

"You're crazy!" Roby exclaimed, dabbing away the blood with a handkerchief.

"You're the one who's crazy," Campagna snarled. "You've used our friendship to make yourself look good in front of your flunkeys, and I'm left looking like a bent cop. I've risked losing everything: reputation, career and pension. What the hell were you thinking of?"

The dealer blushed.

"You know how it is: tongues wag. And I'd had problems with a gang of North Africans who wanted to move in on my territory. I had to say I had your blessing, or I'd never have got them off my back."

Campagna hit him again.

"You bastard, you son of a bitch!"

"That's enough, Giulio! You're smashing my face to a pulp."

"I ought to put a gun in your mouth."

"I'm sorry! I didn't mean to get you into trouble."

"But you did, and it's too late for apologies. You should have told me you were using my name."

"Don't say things like that! We've been friends all our lives."

"We *used to be*," Giulio corrected him caustically. "As far as I'm concerned, you're just a criminal that I've got by the balls now."

Shaken, Pizzo tried to speak, but only managed to nod.

"Where are you meeting your guys?"

"At Eugenio's."

An old restaurant now run by Chinese, who had turned it into a bar that was always deserted.

"Let's get going. You can tell them that from now on you're all under my command."

Pizzo bridled.

"I stopped taking orders when I got the sack. The head of the department was a total dickhead."

The cop lit a cigarette and smoked it halfway.

"You see, Pizzo, I know that you can fuck me over if they put you in jail," he said calmly.

"You can depend on it."

"I would be destroyed. But your little plan makes no allowance for Betta."

"What's my wife got to do with it?"

"Before you open your mouth, I can have her locked up in a jail where girls of a particular kind serve their sentences, and I can call in a few favours that they won't be able to refuse. I assure you that she won't be the same when she comes out, and the rest of your life will be an infinite regret."

Campagna was lying, but Pizzo didn't know he was.

"O.K. then. Let's make a deal, Giulio," he said hastily. "Let's see if we can sort things without doing ourselves any damage."

"Then pull yourself together and answer a few questions. How did my colleague Giacomo Floriani manage to nab Tony Ceccato? It doesn't say in the file."

The dealer delicately touched his nose, which was starting to swell.

"We go to all the motorway petrol stations to sell coke to the lorry drivers. They snort the stuff like drainage pumps so they can keep on driving those beasts day and night," he said. "On Saturdays and Sundays we sell to the drivers parked at the petrol stations. They're knackered, and a bit of coke boosts their morale. A lot of them go in for dogging – you know, husbands bring their wives to be fucked by other guys – and there are a few queers who give blow-jobs like it was going out of fashion."

"What's that got to do with anything?" Campagna snapped.

Pizzo replied in dialect, as he did when he was embarrassed. Tony Ceccato liked the lorry drivers, so he combined pleasure with practicality. One evening in a toilet a man had asked him if he had any coke to sell. When Tony had given him a bag, out had come the man's badge.

"That guy Floriani terrified him," Pizzo added, parking the Punto in front of the bar.

"Tony told Floriani about how you planned to rob Tinko Boyev. Why the Bulgarian Mafia, of all people? Aren't they a bit out of your league?" the policeman asked.

"As I told you, it's our last job. And we have a plant who's supplying us with all the information we need."

"Who is it?"

"The wife of one of the skippers who pilot the boat that carries the cargo. Gigio's been fucking her for a while."

"No-one can keep their trap shut in bed," Campagna observed, getting out of the car.

The two young Chinese men behind the bar did not even glance up when he and Pizzo walked in. Campagna followed Pizzo into the pool room. The other three were there already. Betta, Roby's wife, leapt to her feet when she saw her husband's nose.

"What happened?" she said.

"I elbowed him in the face," the policeman said calmly.

The two heavies, Gigio Marsella and Samuele Lando, got up in turn, their expressions menacing.

"Down, both of you," Campagna commanded, slipping his hand into his jacket.

"Yes, stay calm," Pizzo said. "We need to talk."

After the dealer had brought his gang up to date on the

morning's events, a tense silence fell. Betta broke it before it turned dangerous.

"Explain it to me, Giulio," she asked, in a seemingly calm voice. "We become your little slaves, and, in the end, when you've caught Boyev, you let us go off with the gear?"

"The deal means that you have to leave for good. I never want to see you in the area again. Never."

She played with her lighter for a few seconds before turning back to her husband. "I don't think so. Your friend plans to fuck us over."

"Pizzo isn't my friend anymore," Campagna said harshly. "He's just a treacherous piece of shit. You're not obliged to trust me, but then again you don't really have a choice. As I was just telling your husband, you can land me in the shit once and for all, but I can do worse damage to you. For example, I can have a word with the gang of Albanians you've been thieving from."

"You don't know anything," Gigio exploded.

"What I don't know I'll make up, and your life won't be worth shit," the inspector replied. "But the worst fate is reserved for you, Betta."

"What an honour."

"I've already explained the details to Pizzo." Campagna was not taking the subtle approach. Fear was the only thing that would make them march to his beat. "You're a gang of losers.

You don't have the balls or the funds to play things any differently."

"So what do we have to do?' Pizzo said.

"Tell me everything you know about Boyev's racket, and suspend business until I tell you otherwise."

Dubious glances were exchanged. Then Roby broke in. "Gigio, tell him about this girl you're fucking."

The thug obeyed, and Campagna took his first step into the world of Tinko Boyev.

A few hours later found Campagna waiting for Lopez to wrap up a meeting. Then he made himself comfortable in one of the armchairs in front of Lopez's desk.

"I don't like being this kind of cop," he said.

The head of the flying squad took off his glasses and wiped the lenses with a white handkerchief.

"What do you want me to say, Giulio?"

"Nothing. I just wanted to make sure you'd got your head round the plan."

"I don't understand. You've played dirty before. Like when you planted the coke in that doctor's car, what was her name? Bartolini? She's still doing time in a Slovenian jail."

"She was an accomplice in some horrendous crimes, and she'd have got away with it if I hadn't stopped her."

"And now we're in the same situation with Tinko Boyev, or aren't we?"

"Yes, but this is about playing dirty right down the line. With everybody. Even people who aren't all that guilty will end up paying the price. It's all a bit murky, and not being done by the book."

Lopez unwrapped a sweet and slipped it into his mouth.

"This crap about having to set a good example by not smoking in the office is driving me demented," he complained, sucking noisily.

Campagna reached over and took a sweet wrapped in yellow paper.

"I used to love these honey ones when I was a child."

They stared at each other for a few seconds.

"Our world has changed since cocaine arrived, you know. We've already had this discussion," Lopez said.

"It's true. You're right."

"So I hope you're not planning on pulling out of this one," Lopez said. "Because I wouldn't know how to save you."

"But if I fuck Boyev over, I can say I turned a blind eye to the activities of Pizzo's gang in order to get my hands on the Bulgarians."

"Nobody would bat an eye, though it won't be easy for you to collect evidence without wire taps or help from the guys in forensics."

"I'd already worked that out."

"Then we're clear."

The inspector got to his feet.

"Once the case is closed, I want to be transferred to Robberies."

"Fine, Giulio. I promise."

Leaving the station, Campagna strolled to Piazza delle Erbe, where he drank a prosecco and had a bite to eat. He was playing for time. He needed to act, but he had no desire to do so. He crossed the centre of town and reached the architect's office where his wife worked. He felt the need to confide in her, something he always did at difficult times. This was particularly difficult.

Her secretary informed him that Gaia had gone to check on a building site and would not be returning to the office. Taking that as a sign, Campagna went back to the station.

"I need a few hundred grams of coke from reserves," he said to Pinamonti.

"What are you going to do with it?"

"You really want to know?"

Pinamonti raised his hands in a gesture of surrender.

"No! I'm up to my eyes in my own shit, and yours is usually deeper."

The inspector looked at him with genuine astonishment.

"Where do you get these ridiculous phrases from?"

"That one wasn't bad, was it?" Pinamonti said, defending himself. He opened a safe containing various confiscated but unrecorded items. "I'd say it's evocative in a way that's brilliant and refined at the same time."

"You're right," Campagna joked. "Use it on the boss next time you deliver a report."

"No, I reserve my comments for those who can appreciate them," Pinamonti said seriously, handing him a bag of cocaine. "That's 257 grams. Will that do?"

"That'll do just fine."

Twenty minutes later Campagna rang the bell of a flat in a 1970s working-class block as ugly as the five others that loomed around it. The countryside was not far away, and hordes of little villas crowded in from all directions

The door was opened by a woman of about fifty. Tall, stout, hatchet-faced. She glanced distractedly at the policeman's badge.

"I'm the housekeeper, and my papers are in order, she informed him abruptly in a strong eastern European accent.

"I'm looking for Tony."

"He's watching television with his mum."

The woman led Campagna to the sitting room. The house smelled stale: of food, cats and old age.

Tony was slouching in an old armchair covered with a red-and-white plaid blanket. He was stroking an obese cat curled up in his lap as he watched a programme in which elderly men and women wooed one another without realising how ridiculous they looked.

His old mother was sitting in a wheelchair. It only took Campagna a moment to realise that while her legs might not have been able to support her anymore, her mind was fully present.

"Who are you?" she asked in a strong Paduan accent.

"He's a policeman," the housekeeper said quickly.

Tony had not bothered to get up. He had recognised the policeman as Pizzo's friend, and in his new role as Floriani's informer he thought he had nothing to fear.

"Hello," the inspector said politely, before turning to the seated man. "Come with me, Tony. We need to talk."

The dealer set the cat delicately on the floor and got up.

"Fine," he said calmly. "I'll get my jacket and be with you in a second."

"What's he done this time?" his mother asked.

"I can't tell you that, Madam," the inspector said.

"It's about men again, isn't it?" the woman insisted bitterly. "Even you know that Tony's homosexual. But not one of those guys who stick it in other men's arseholes; he's like a woman. The only reason he doesn't wear a skirt is because he's ugly as sin."

"Stop it, Mamma," her son said wearily.

"You must know, my dear sir, that it was Tony's fault that my husband died of a broken heart," Signora Ceccato continued undeterred, not even stopping to draw breath. "He's an only child, so he's left me without grandchildren. We were manual workers, and we couldn't afford more than one kid because when I fell pregnant the boss sacked me and I had to find a new job ten kilometres away, and I got frostbite riding my bike in the winter."

"That's your business, Signora; I'm not interested." Campagna tried to shut her up, but the woman was like a river in flood. She had a lousy life story to offload onto whoever would listen.

"I pay my taxes, and this government of swindlers is robbing me blind. You've got to listen to me because I pay your wages, don't I?"

"Another time," the policeman muttered, pushing the dealer out of the room. "It's none of my business, but why do you still live with your mum when she treats you like that?" he asked.

Tony had pale blue eyes, a round face and a flaccid, overweight body. He looked down at his shoes and didn't reply.

The inspector wondered why on earth Pizzo had made the person least likely to dedicate himself to crime a part of his gang. Perhaps so that he could go on protecting him after he left the trade union. Now Campagna was going to ruin Tony for ever by throwing him in jail. It was his only option if he was to gain time on Floriani.

"Where are we going?" Tony said, once they'd got into the car.

"To the station. You're under arrest."

Tony turned white as a sheet.

"What for? I haven't done anything."

Campagna took the bag of coke out of his jacket pocket.

"Possession with intent to supply 257 grams of 87 per cent pure cocaine."

"But it isn't mine," the man whined.

"It is now. I just found it in your jacket pocket," Campagna said, taking out his handcuffs.

"Please talk to Floriani. He'll tell you to let me go."

Campagna breathed in deeply, trying to find the strength to be ruthless with the poor wretch. Pressing his pistol to the man's cheek, he brought his mouth to his ear.

"You've got to stop talking to my colleague, or I'll put a rumour about in jail that you're a snitch, and it won't just be cocks they're shoving up your arse, it'll be table legs."

Tony burst into tears. He was inconsolable; it was pitiful to watch. The cop was forced to punch him in the stomach to make him stop. It was important for him to take the threat on board.

"And then I'll go and talk to the Albanians you've robbed, and send them to pay a little visit to your mother."

"No, not Mamma! Leave her alone, I beg you! I'll do whatever you want!"

Campagna put the pistol back in its holster and set off. In the course of the journey he explained exactly what he wanted Tony to do. When they reached the courtyard of the station, Tony begged him again not to hurt his mother.

I don't want to be this kind of a cop, Giulio thought for the umpteenth time as he got out of the car.

When Floriani found out about Ceccato's arrest, he tore into Campagna like a Fury.

"You think you're smart," he shouted. "But I'm going to be on your case until I can prove you're in cahoots with your pal Pizzo."

The inspector replied by grabbing hold of him, and the commotion attracted the interest of Lopez, who came out of his office.

"That's enough," he thundered. His authority was sufficient to calm everyone down. Then he pointed to Sovrintendente Capo Floriani. "Come here, Giacomo. We need to have a word."

Campagna's hands were shaking. He knew what was going to happen, but he found it hard to accept his colleague's accusations.

"It's all a big mistake," Pinamonti said loudly, coming to his aid. "It'll sort itself out. You'll see."

Linking arms with the inspector, Pinamonti walked him to the station canteen.

"What the fuck happened?" he asked, once they were safe from flapping ears.

"I arrested one of Floriani's informers. I messed up one of his investigations."

"With that quarter-kilo I gave you a while back?"

"Yes."

"Why did you go and do something stupid like that?"

Campagna looked him straight in the eye.

"You really want to know?"

"Am I going to end up in the shit?"

"No."

Pinamonti took a step back, stirring a cup of coffee.

"Then I'm not interested, Giulio. It's your business, and given that you're not bent, it will sort itself out."

When they got back to the office they found Floriani waiting for Campagna. Offering the inspector his hand, he apologised in front of their colleagues. It was obvious that he was doing so under Lopez's orders. Campagna could read it in his eyes, which looked icy. This was exactly what he had expected when he had arrested Tony Ceccato, but he tightened his grip and whispered, "You and I need to have a chat."

"Can't wait," Floriani growled, and walked away, his heels clattering.

Campagna realised that Lopez had ordered Floriani not to get in his way. That clearly was not enough for Floriani, who was now risking the operation by becoming a loose cannon. For the umpteenth time he cursed Roby Pizzo and his stupid big mouth.

Gigio Marsella was a hundred per cent certain. Lidia Guolo never missed a show by the U.B. Dolls. Campagna had attended a few performances by those four wild girls, who had sold their souls to rockabilly. In fact he had liked them so much that he had bought their last C.D., which Ilaria had immediately pinched. The dealer had given him a photograph of Lidia taken with his mobile so that the inspector would recognise her: a peroxide blonde of about thirty, scantily dressed and very pretty. She had a chic hairdo, and her earrings clearly came from a very elegant boutique. She did not seem to have anything in common with Gigio, who was a great hairy lump of a thing with features typical of the Veneto.

That evening the group were performing in a bar in the province of Rovigo. The inspector came in just as the U.B. Dolls were launching into "Stupid Cupid", an old hit sung by Connie Francis, which his mother had liked a lot. He ordered a beer and walked towards the stage. He remembered that the guitarist, who went by the name of Jeky Kalashnikov, was not only a good singer but pretty as well. He enjoyed listening to "Daddy Sang Bass" in an arrangement very different from Johnny Cash's version, and then he went in search of Lidia Guolo.

He found her sitting with a friend. They were drinking bourbon on the rocks, and like real fans they were savouring every note. Campagna needed to speak to her alone, so he resigned himself to waiting. After a while her friend got up and headed for the toilet. The cop quickly took her place.

"There's someone sitting there," the woman said, not deigning to look at him.

"I know. Your friend went to powder her nose. I bet you didn't go with her so that you wouldn't lose your table, but you can't wait to snort a nice big line of coke yourself."

"Fuck off, dickhead."

When the cop discreetly showed his badge, the woman turned pale enough to suggest that there was sufficient cocaine in her handbag to land her in serious trouble.

"Do you deal or just use?" Campagna went on.

"A line every now and then," she stammered, her back to the wall. "I don't deal, I swear."

"You don't need to, given that your husband transports it by the ton in that lovely little boat of his."

Lidia Guolo shook her head.

"That's not true. Luca's just a skipper."

"We've just arrested him," the inspector lied.

That's impossible! He's in Croatia visiting his father."

"The Croatian police have brought him to the border," Campagna said, getting to his feet. "Come on, I'm taking you to the station to give a statement."

"But what about my friend?"

"She can stay and enjoy the gig."

Crushed, the woman allowed herself to be led through the deserted car park, where Campagna handcuffed her and confiscated her mobile phone before shoving her into the boot of his car.

Lidia Guolo did not have the strength to yell for help.

Campagna drove along minor roads to a small villa that had been confiscated from a dealer a few months previously, and for which he had a duplicate set of keys. Often the station was not the ideal place to question suspects who might be turned into informers, and having empty houses ready for the purpose had become common practice for cops like him.

Campagna hid the car in the garage, which connected directly to the kitchen. He let the woman out of the boot and she, still in shock, did not react. Removing the cuffs, he sat her down in one of the armchairs in the sitting room.

"Call Luca," he said, giving her back her mobile.

"And tell him what?"

"Tell him what's just happened to you and then pass him over to me."

The woman nodded, but at the sound of her husband's voice she burst into tears, unable to get a single word out. Sighing, Campagna grabbed the phone from her hand.

"Lidia! Lidia! What's going on?" her husband shouted.

"I've got her," the inspector said.

"And who the fuck are you?"

"Let me speak to your father."

"I asked you who the fuck you are!"

"Someone who's got your wife and wants to talk to your father and not to you because you're an insignificant prick."

The telephone was passed over.

"Alessandro de Simone speaking."

A deep, authoritative voice. It was branded on the inspector's memory. Like all the other failures in his life and career.

"Campagna. Remember me?"

"How could I forget, when it's your fault I'm here?"

Gun-running during the war in the former Yugoslavia. de Simone and the Brenta Mafia had supplied the Croatians with heavy arms via a man from Verona who worked for the German secret service. A complicated exchange of favours that brought in a whole lot of money. Campagna had worked on the investigation that would have nailed the lot of them if other servants of the state, secret and powerful, had not intervened and buried the whole affair. Alessandro de Simone had been given asylum in Croatia. Since then, he had not moved, abandoning his wife and son in Italy. At least that was what he had led people to believe. It was not difficult to imagine that peace and geopolitical stability would lead him towards other kinds of trafficking, of which the cocaine trade was one of the most profitable. But the trafficker had been careful not to provide any leads. When Gigio Marsella had told him that the lovely Lidia was married to Luca de Simone, however, the inspector had put two and two together, and come up with a plan.

"I've got your daughter-in-law," Campagna said.

"Have you arrested her?"

"No."

"What are you going to do with her?"

"I need her to get to your son. And to you," the cop said.

"Assuming she talks."

Campagna burst out laughing.

"She's sleeping with a guy from a rival gang, and she's told him tons of things she learned from Luca already. You're doing business with a bunch of idiots."

He clearly heard both the slap that de Simone gave his son and the son's whining protests.

"What do you want?" the trafficker said.

"This time it won't be the cops who save you. You're risking extradition, my friend."

"I asked you what the fuck you want!" de Simone yelled.

"Tinko Boyev."

When the trafficker didn't reply, Campagna took advantage of his silence to play another trump card.

"I've drawn up a chart of the gang, and Lidia's a credible witness. Boyev isn't going to be at all happy that an arrangement shifting 2,000 kilos a month has been blown sky-high thanks to your son, because that's exactly what I'm going to tell him tomorrow."

"You don't think I'm going to talk about this on the phone, do you?"

"Of course not. Send me your son so that we can make a deal."

"How do I know I can trust you, cop?"

"Sleep on it. And give me an answer tomorrow."

Turning off his telephone, Campagna looked at Lidia, who was staring at him wide-eyed. She was terrified.

"He'll kill me," she whispered.

"Your father-in-law?"

"Yes."

Taking her by the arm, he sat her down at the dining table and placed a pen and pad of paper in front of her.

"Start writing," he ordered.

"What?"

"The answers to my questions."

This was the system used by police in America; Campagna had learned it from watching *NYPD Blue*. Suspects were always asked to write out their statements; once they had been set down in their own handwriting, they were harder to deny. He badly needed confessions to produce at the right moment. He might neglect to mention that the witness had been kidnapped and interrogated at a secret location, though.

Three hours later, the inspector was aghast. Lidia Guolo knew a lot, too much just to have learned it from her husband, and she had written a full confession, more useful than he could ever have imagined it would be. She had only told Gigio a very small part of it. She confessed that she had a lover and that she had waved the plan for a doomed robbery under his nose because she was afraid that he would lose interest in her otherwise.

"How come you fancy someone like Marsella?"

"He's not a pussy like Luca."

"So you don't think your husband's much of a man?"

"Only on his boat. In everyday life he's deadly boring."

"But your marriage is over," Campagna said. "And, now that I think of it, so's your affair with Gigio."

"Why? We're good together."

"He wants to end it."

"How do you know?"

"I ordered him to."

"Bastard!" she sobbed.

"It's for the best. You're about to go on journeys that will separate you for ever."

Locking the woman in the cellar, Campagna drove back to Padua with her confession in his inside jacket pocket. When he turned his mobile back on, he found a stream of messages and calls from Gaia. He called her.

"It's 4.00 in the morning!" his wife yelled hysterically. "Do you want me to die of anxiety?"

"Sorry, Gaia! I'm in the middle of an operation and I forgot to tell you."

"When will you be back?"

"I don't know. As soon as possible."

"You didn't even take your toothbrush!"

"I didn't have time."

"Oh fuck off, Giulio, just fuck off!" Gaia exploded. "Your colleagues always tell their wives. You're the only one who forgets. Is that how much your family means to you?"

When she slammed down the telephone, Campagna vented his frustration by punching the steering wheel. Berating himself, he stopped at an all-night bar for a sandwich. At 5.00 a.m. he called Pinamonti.

"Couldn't you have let me sleep for another few hours?"

"I need to talk to Floriani straight away."

"Then call him."

"He wouldn't pick up for me, Damiano. You talk to him, please."

"O.K."

Two cigarettes later Campagna's phone started to vibrate.

"Floriani here."

"I need to see you."

"Where are you?"

"Padua south."

"I'll see you in half an hour at the first rest stop on the motorway to Bologna."

The inspector arrived first and had two cups of coffee. Only then did he realise that he had not slept in a long time and that his thoughts were starting to blur. He bought a pack of cigarettes and sat where he could be seen. Floriani arrived in a cheap car that perfectly suited the role he was playing.

Campagna opened the door and got in. Then handed Floriani Lidia Guolo's confession.

"I owe you an explanation, but first I want you to read this."

Making himself comfortable, Floriani put on a pair of reading glasses.

"You want me to take this to a judge and set up an official investigation, is that right?" he said after he had finished reading.

"Yes."

"While you . . ."

"Go after Boyev."

"Why?"

"He killed a friend of mine," Campagna lied.

Floriani waved a hand in the air.

"Oh come on, Campagna, I know very well that the colleague killed by Boyev wasn't a friend of yours."

"What difference does that make?"

Floriani shrugged.

"None at all, but don't treat me like an idiot. Now tell me about your links with Pizzo's gang."

Campagna told him almost everything.

"I don't want them to get away with it," Floriani said sonorously. "I'm going to take them down."

"Perhaps we could offer them some mitigation," the inspector suggested.

"Fine. You're right, they're a bunch of losers, but dealing cocaine is still a crime."

"So I can count you in?"

"Yes."

"Then I'll give you Lidia Guolo and you can decide what to do with her."

Floriani tapped the papers.

"I will certainly put the squeeze on her. This is too detailed a confession to make me think she based it all on things her husband told her."

Campagna smiled.

"Lidia is an active member of the gang. I haven't the slightest doubt about that. She's acting the fool, grassing up everyone else to save her own skin."

"And in the end that's what she'll do. But I don't understand why she's connected to someone like Gigio Marsella."

"She probably wanted to persuade him to do something for her."

"Eliminate her husband and nick a whole cargo. As the skipper's wife she had access to the boat whenever she wanted."

"That's how she managed to escape her father-in-law's influence. But I let the cat out of the bag yesterday, and de Simone has a long memory. Lidia Guolo is destined for witness protection, if she wants to save her skin. By the way, I'm glad we've sorted things out, Giacomo. I couldn't bear the idea of people thinking I was a bent cop."

"I'm sorry, but there was all that evidence ..."

"When this is over, I'm going back to robberies," the inspector said.

"That's good news," his colleague said. "You're not cut out for the drugs squad."

"You reckon?"

"Yes. You're one of those cops that need precise boundaries," he said.

"A robbery is a clearly defined crime, and relationships with criminals are clearly defined too."

"Drug trafficking used to be like that," the inspector objected.

"You're right, but in those days there were only traffickers and cops. Normal people hadn't got involved, the ones who should never start playing cops-and-robbers. Like your friend Pizzo. They're the ones who messed everything up."

Campagna lit a cigarette, lost in thought. His colleague did not interrupt him. They drove to the villa, where Floriani took delivery of Lidia Guolo. Campagna gripped her by the shoulders.

"We've decided to stick with your game, but you have to stick with ours too."

"What does that mean?"

"That you've got to act out the script written by my colleague here."

The woman nodded, smiling fatuously.

"I think I can do that."

"I'm sure you will, gorgeous," the inspector said.

Watching her leave with Floriani, Campagna turned the woman's mobile back on. Then he went and found a bed to get some sleep. The telephone woke him late in the afternoon.

"I decided not to trust you," de Simone said. "My son's staying here with me."

"You did the right thing," Campagna said. "Your daughter-in-law wrote out a long confession. She's sold you to us at a knock-down price."

"You made a big mistake choosing that bitch rather than using me to get to Boyev."

"No way. As I told you before, I'm going to make sure Tinko believes that you were the ones who stole from him and takes his revenge as only he knows how. I've read that his speciality is three knitting needles in the liver, guaranteeing a long and painful death. But you know that already, or else you wouldn't have bothered to call."

"Don't even think about trying to scare me with this bullshit, cop," de Simone sneered. "I have more experience than you when it comes to this sort of thing."

"I've always thought you had blood on your hands, and I'm glad to hear you confirming as much."

The trafficker ignored him.

"I've reached the conclusion that taking out Boyev is everybody's business. Perhaps I can hand him over to you along with his right-hand man in Padua, but I need a guarantee that you've understood what I've been saying."

"You say 'taking out'," Giulio said. "That concept is as clear to me as it can be to a policeman in a constitutional democracy."

de Simone ignored him again. That bloody cop was still trying to provoke him. "How long have we got before the operation starts?"

"I don't know, but I don't think it'll be long."

"I need you to let me know in advance."

"You're asking a lot, given that you don't trust me."

"It's the only way I can hand Tinko over to you."

Campagna hung up, racked with doubt. Was he really up to mounting an operation with criminals of this calibre on his own?

Ilaria hugged him.

"Dad, you stink!" she exclaimed, but still held him tight.

"You're right, sweetie! I'm about to take a shower. Where's Mum?"

"Still at work. She told me to beat you up when you came home."

"So you're disobeying your mother."

"That's what she'll think."

"Is she really cross?"

"And she's right as usual. You always behave badly."

Campagna pulled away from his daughter.

"I knew it!" he exploded, starting to unbutton his shirt. He had only just got home and already he needed a change of air. His wife and daughter would make him pay dearly, and he might as well get used to it.

In fact he was wrong. Gaia acted as if nothing had happened, merely avoiding any expressions of affection. At least that was Giulio's initial impression. He immediately fell asleep in front of the television, during a programme about the kidnapping of a surveyor linked to a dodgy politician. The thugs involved were so pitiful that they made Roby Pizzo and his gang look great.

"With all the stuff we have to do, and we're wasting time on crap like this," he remembered saying to his wife, before slipping into a deep sleep.

The next morning he got to the office more or less on time. Pinamonti was waiting for him.

"Did you sort things out with Floriani?"

"Yes, it's all fine, Damiano. Thanks for your intervention."

"I was sure it would be O.K.," Pinamonti said. "Because I understand your characters. You're like two planets that cannot interact."

"Lay off!" the inspector exclaimed indignantly. "That's not

fair first thing in the morning! Be careful, Damiano. You may be my boss, but I can still get you sent to the police shrink, and she takes no prisoners!"

On his way to the canteen, Campagna was intercepted by an old acquaintance, a lawyer by the name of Ravasi. A woman in her fifties, she was a good defence attorney, had a passion for hopeless cases and wanted to talk to him about one of them.

"Can I buy you a coffee?" Campagna said.

"Of course, *ispettore.*"

"What dreadful fuck-up have I created this time?' the policeman asked, as they waited in the queue for the till.

"Tony Ceccato," Ravasi said. "I'm trying to have him put under house arrest. He won't survive in prison. He'll kill himself."

"Have you met his mother? Honestly I don't know which option is preferable for Tony."

"I haven't met her, no, but she can't be worse than a prison cell," the woman said, resting her hand on his arm.

"I'll have a word with the judge," Campagna promised.

He went straight to the prosecutor, Nunziata, to try to rid himself of his sense of guilt about Ceccato. He had handed Tony in because his arrest was strategically necessary if Campagna was to block Floriani's investigation. But now, with that matter resolved, keeping him in jail would be doubly mean.

"I've fucked up, Nunziata," he said.

"Excuse me, but is that the appropriate way to express yourself in front of a magistrate?"

"I've arrested a colleague's informer by mistake."

"Are you referring to Antonio Ceccato, known as Tony?"

"Yes."

"So much the worse for you. What do you want me to do?"

"Put him under house arrest."

"I'll review the case in a month or so."

"He'll hang himself first!"

"Fine! Take more care in future."

Late that afternoon Campagna met Floriani at the rest-stop café on the motorway to Bologna.

"Why do you like hanging out here? What's so interesting about it?" the inspector asked.

"I'm looking for a truck-driver carrying drugs and weapons," Floriani replied. "He's a Turk. I've only ever seen him once, but I'll never forget his face. I've set him a trap, and I hope he's going to fall into it."

"What's he done to you?"

Picking up his wallet, Floriani took out a bit of knife-blade broken about three centimetres from the tip.

"This is the souvenir that he left between my ribs."

"When you find him and need help, remember that I'm at your disposal."

"Thanks, I'll bear that in mind."

"Any news about the Bulgarian gang?"

"It's actually Bulgarian–Italian," Floriani said, and started to talk about how Tinko Boyev had set up in Padua thanks to the presence there of a distant cousin who had provided him with his first operational base. In the early days, the cocaine had arrived by land, but then the Bulgarian mafioso had heard about de Simone and his skill with organising marine transport when he was involved in arms trafficking. So they had met up and liked each other. The gang was born. There were now different bases around the city, each supplying a particular region. Turnover was considerable, given that they brought in at least 2,000 kilos of cocaine every month.

de Simone Senior set up a small fleet of merchant ships that handed over the goods off the Italian coast, transferring them to three sailing boats operated by his son Luca, who relied on the complicity of two further skippers and a few sailors, all above suspicion and with clean records.

"And it would all have gone on working with the precision of a Swiss watch," Giulio said, "if Lidia Guolo hadn't gone to bed with Gigio Marsella and said things she shouldn't have."

Floriani took a bite from a sandwich he had purchased.

"That's how most investigations start. A phrase, a

confidence, a fling. Then we show up. By the way," he said, his mouth full of sandwich, "we're going to arrest them all tomorrow morning."

"No-one told me."

"Lopez wanted to keep you out of it. He said you were busy with another investigation, so I took it that the order to get Boyev at all costs came straight from him."

Campagna shrugged.

"You know I can't give you an answer, but I can tell you that the next few hours are going to be hell, because I've got a bloody hard decision to make."

Floriani shook his hand.

"Good luck. No point my saying that I don't envy you at all."

Campagna could not take that horrible decision, but neither could he stand still. Driving back and forth along the motorways that criss-crossed the city, he risked several collisions because his head was elsewhere. He called Gaia.

"Don't tell me you're on site or with clients, because I need you."

"I'm hungry," she said calmly. "And I fancy a steak. Will you take me to Athos?"

"If there's a table, of course I will."

"Book one, then. Threaten to arrest them all if they make a fuss."

There was a table. Given the economic crisis, people thought twice before splashing out, even though the food and wine were worth it.

Gaia really was a beautiful woman, Giulio thought, watching her as she ate. He wondered if she was happy being with him. They had been through so much. Some of it seriously bad, some less so, but now they seemed to have achieved a kind of equilibrium. Ilaria was growing up, but he himself was not. He would never get any better. It was too late.

Gaia looked up and smiled. Giulio took advantage of the moment.

"I've an appointment with a low-life who's supposed to call me, but if he cheats it's going to scupper a huge operation."

"And?" his wife cut in.

"And a lot else besides, including my career."

Gaia locked her fingers together beneath her chin in a gesture that Campagna thought revealed her innate elegance.

"'Normal' people have a heap of problems weighing them down and making their lives complicated. Sometimes it's a real mess," she said in a low voice. "But policemen aren't 'normal', because, apart from their own problems, they face other ones, often insurmountable, which have to do with life, death and freedom."

"I don't understand what you're getting at, Gaia."

"You've got to follow your instincts. You've been doing this job for so long. Just trust your intuition and your experience," she said with a melancholy smile. "Sorry, but all these things make me terribly anxious, and I can't share them with you because they're none of my business. You should know that by now."

"I'm the one who's sorry. I didn't want to involve you in all this," Giulio said hastily, as if he had just been slapped. "And I have been exaggerating. You know what I'm like. I prefer to think of myself at the heart of really important issues, when in fact they're just the usual crap that provincial cops have to deal with."

Gaia took his hand and gripped it tightly.

"Follow your instinct, and don't worry about me," she cut him short. "And now, I fancy that hot chocolate fondant. How about you have the crème caramel and we share?"

It was at that moment that the inspector decided to call de Simone.

Using the excuse of a quick cigarette, he left the restaurant and switched on Lidia Guolo's phone.

"Tomorrow at dawn," he said in one breath before hanging up.

Alessandro de Simone turned up a few hours later.

"This is how it's going to be: tonight I'll warn Stoyàn, my cousin, that the cops are coming, and tell him where to hide. Then he'll put me in touch with Tinko, and I'll tell Tinko where to find him. The rest is up to you."

Campagna was disappointed. It sounded like a rotten plan.

"Tinko Boyev is an important businessman in his own country. Why should he take personal risks? He has an army of henchmen."

The trafficker snorted impatiently.

"You only say that because you don't know the guy. Tinko is first and foremost a Bulgarian mafioso, and he won't think for a minute about entrusting the safety of a first cousin to a stranger. You'll see. He'll turn up armed to the teeth with Anton, his right-hand man, who's his nephew – another bloody relative."

In the face of such vehemence, the inspector said nothing.

"Where's the hiding-place?" he asked.

"On the outskirts of Abano Terme. A newly built block with four empty flats. The area's ideal because it's isolated, nobody ever goes there, and it's practically the countryside. I'll text you the address."

Once he had the address, the inspector hurried to check out the block of flats. It was a perfect place to hide, but also perfect for what he had been thinking about for a few days. He did not dare to call it a plan, because he had not yet decided what his own role was going to be.

For once he arrived at his office early. The drugs section was in party mood, and everyone was excited ahead of the mid-morning press conference. The Bulgarian–Italian gang had been destroyed, and all its affiliates – except Anton Boyev and Luca de Simone – had been arrested in various cities in the north. Almost 300 kilos of cocaine, a load of cash and several properties had been confiscated.

The interrogations were in full swing. None of the Paduan suspects had ever had a run-in with the law before. They had clean records and were in regular employment.

Giulio bumped into Floriani and congratulated him with a slap on the shoulder.

"Have you made a decision?" his colleague asked.

"Yes, but I have to make certain that it's the right one."

He joined in with the general euphoria for a few minutes, then sneaked off and went down to the armoury.

"I need two reserve magazines," he told the man in charge.

His colleague did not object, and asked him to sign the register before handing over thirty 9 mm Parabellum bullets.

Campagna left the station and phoned Roby Pizzo.

"Today's the big day," he announced. "Call your boys, but leave the lady at home. I don't want her getting shot."

They met at Eugenio's. Campagna showed up with a tablet containing the photographs he had taken with his mobile phone of the refuge where Tinko Boyev's fugitive cousin was hiding and the surrounding area.

"In that house there's about 30 kilos of cocaine that Stoyàn has managed to save, but, more importantly, there's about 500,000 euros in cash."

He was lying shamelessly; even though it was likely that Stoyàn had probably not fled empty-handed, it was still a shameless lie.

"The Bulgarian is alone, but the doors and windows are armour-plated. It's impossible to get in. You have to wait for the others to turn up and collect him. A car carrying two people is going to turn up, he'll get out and collect the bags of drugs and cash, and only then can you pounce and get him."

"And you have no idea when they'll get there?" Samuele said.

"Could be any time, though it's likely that they'll show up tonight."

"They'll be armed to the teeth, with their fingers on their triggers," Gigio observed. "This time we have to take into account the possibility of a gunfight."

"Those are the risks you take when there's money involved," Pizzo broke in. "More than we've ever seen before."

"And you'll have a tidy sum to emigrate with," the inspector added, hoping with all his might that Pizzo was not about to change his mind.

"Putting Tony in jail was a crap idea," Gigio said.

"A few days and he'll be under house arrest," Campagna said. "I had to jail him to block my colleague's investigation. Otherwise Tony would have told him everything he knew. Otherwise we'd have been up to our necks in shit."

He got to his feet.

"Once this job is finished, get the hell out."

Roby Pizzo and his men turned up near the block of flats. They were driving three cars which they had stolen and kept in safe garages after putting on new plates. They took up strategic positions and settled down to wait, staying in contact by mobile phone. A little way off, Betta waited in the clean car that they were going to use for their getaway. Pizzo had refused to listen to Campagna and involved her in the raid.

Just before midnight a big black 4x4 arrived. It stopped a short distance away and its headlights were turned off. A while later the porch light of the house lit up, and a man with a bag and a big trolley came outside. Only then was the car started again, crawling slowly forward.

Everything happened in a flash. The three cars came out of their hiding-places and surrounded the 4x4. But Pizzo and his men were not professionals, and had no idea what to do in the face of bursts of machine-gun fire muted by silencers. Roby Pizzo and Samuele went down in a matter of seconds. Only Gigio managed to get out of the car and fire his revolver at the 4x4 before Stoyàn, the fugitive, peppered his chest with bullets.

The 4x4 was trapped, though, and its two occupants had to get out to help extricate it. At that moment Campagna emerged from the darkness and opened fire. He emptied the magazine, reloaded and fired the same number of bullets again at the Bulgarians. He was sure he had hit two of them, but when the third one started returning fire with his machine-gun Campagna retreated into the darkness.

Hearing sirens in the distance, he imagined that the *carabinieri* from the barracks in Abano Terme must be on their way and ran faster. There was no plausible explanation he could offer them.

Next morning, as he was shaving, Campagna listened to an item on the radio about a gun battle between drug traffickers in a quiet provincial town near Padua, which had led to the deaths of four men, the wounding of one and the arrest of the fugitive Stoyàn Boyev. His cousin Tinko, suspected for some time of being a leading figure in the Bulgarian Mafia, had been identified among the victims. The wounded man turned out to be Anton, Tinko's nephew.

When Giulio walked into the office, he was told that the boss was looking for him.

"You've been transferred to Robberies," Lopez said flatly. "You start tomorrow. You'll spend today handing over to your colleagues here."

No mention of the death of Boyev, or of his avenged colleague. Not even an exchange of glances.

Campagna did not obey his boss's orders and left the

station instead. He had other plans. First he went to see Betta, Roby Pizzo's wife.

"I've come to tell you you're not going to jail," he said. "That's all I can do for you."

"You had him killed," the widow muttered.

"They knew the risks they were taking. No-one forced them."

Then he went to the hospital. Pinamonti, Floriani and some other colleagues were standing outside the ward to which Anton Boyev had been brought, talking animatedly about the shooting. Police regulation cartridges had been found at the site. Although that information would certainly not be passed to journalists, it did raise questions about how a police revolver had found its way into the hands of the criminals.

"How is the Bulgarian?" Campagna said.

"A bullet in the hip, nothing serious," Pinamonti said.

"Can I go in for a moment?"

"Why?"

"I just want to have a quick look," he murmured. "I've had an idea that I want to check out."

"Be my guest," said Pinamonti. "You might even be able to make him talk."

Entering the room, campagna went straight over to the bed and brought his mouth to the mafioso's ear.

"Alessandro de Simone betrayed you," he whispered in very bad English.

Anton Boyev acted as if he had not understood.

Campagna left the room and stayed with the others until the magistrate arrived with an interpreter.

"I'm moving to Robberies," he told Pinamonti and Floriani.

Pinamonti was lost for words and slightly offended at having been kept in the dark about his friend's request for a transfer.

But Giacomo complimented him. Then he added in a low voice, "As I said, you're not really cut out for the drugs squad. You're an alchemist who stirs things up so that they produce phenomena. Like that gun battle last night, which had your signature all over it."

"Are you referring to the bullets? It was important for the message to get through loud and clear to the Bulgarians: You don't kill cops. I also promised Pizzo's widow that she's not going to end up in jail."

"You did the right thing."

Finally, Campagna turned on his phone and called Alessandro de Simone.

"Now we're sorted," the drug trafficker said.

"I am. You aren't."

"What the hell's that supposed to mean?"

"I just told Anton Boyev you were the one who betrayed him. You and your son better get going because the Bulgarians are about to declare open season on you."

"What did you do that for?" de Simone stammered.

"Because otherwise you'd be the only ones to get away scot-free while everyone else in this business has paid a price. And also, de Simone, because some old scores are being settled."

"You're a dead man, Campagna. I'm going to slaughter your whole family," the trafficker said in a confused babble.

"If you want to save yourself and give your son a future, you should get to the border. I can be there in two hours."

"Alessandro isn't a traitor."

"Perhaps he is," Campagna said. "At any rate I'm going to leave my phone on, so when you're ready, call me."

The Speed of the Angel

GIANRICO CAROFIGLIO

Translated by Howard Curtis

I LIKE WRITING IN CAFÉS. IT'S AN OLD OBSESSION OF MINE, starting from when I was young and read Hemingway and thought working in public places was an absolute prerequisite for becoming a writer.

I stopped reading Hemingway some years ago, and even found the courage to say that, truth be told, I don't like him all that much. Some of his novels are actually quite boring – sometimes *very* boring. But I've kept up the habit of writing in cafés.

It was a late afternoon in September. The place – I don't know if it still exists – was called the Caffè del Pescatore and had no particular attractions, apart from a little terrace with a view of the breakwater and the sea, and the almost total absence of other customers.

I sat down, ordered a glass of chilled white wine, opened my laptop and started writing. When I work in my study, I get

distracted every five minutes, whereas in public places, I somehow, mysteriously, find it easier to concentrate and can write
for a long time, barely aware of the passing hours.

I resurfaced from my work after an indeterminate length
of time, two glasses of wine, and a plate of *taralli*, olives and
provolone. Meanwhile, a couple of other tables had been occupied. Directly in front of me were two young men dressed in
black from head to toe, smoking smelly cigarettes, drinking
beer and eating French fries.

Sitting to my right was a woman wearing cargo trousers
and a white T-shirt. She had the fit body of an athlete – lean,
with slender, muscular arms and broad shoulders – but her face
was marked by lines like razor scars, horizontal on the forehead,
vertical at the sides of her mouth.

On her table were a beer, a bread roll and a spiral notebook.
She was writing something with the syncopated haste of
someone trying to keep hold of a thought, afraid it might
escape. She stopped after a time, took a bite of her bread roll
and a sip of beer, then started writing again. She exuded a
mixture of self-control, urgency and instability, and also – it
took me a while to identify this – a vague sense of menace. It
was impossible not to look at her.

After a while she stood up to stretch her legs. As she raised
one knee towards her chest, a handful of coins fell out of her
trouser pocket. They hit the floor like a brief burst of gunfire,

and quite a few of them rolled under my chair. I stood up to help her collect them.

"Thanks," she said as we stood facing each other, halfway between her table and mine.

"Why do you carry so much small change?" I asked for no particular reason, just to have something to say, but she seemed to take the question seriously. She let a few seconds pass, weighing it up, then decided to reply.

"They're for beggars."

"What do you mean?"

"I always carry a few coins to give to beggars."

"Just like Matthew Scudder."

"Who's he?"

"He's the main character in a series of novels set in New York. An ex-policeman who's become a private investigator. He does the same thing. Whenever he gets paid for a job, he changes part of the money into dollar bills to give to any beggars he might come across."

"An ex-policeman," she said slowly, as if she had never heard the expression before and had to think carefully about its meaning.

"Yes. Do you know the novels?"

"No." She paused for a long time, looking at me as if searching for something that escaped her. "Are they a kind of crime fiction?"

"Yes."

"Crime fiction isn't my favourite. To be honest, I never read it."

"What do you read?"

"Whatever I come across. I'm trying to catch up."

"Catch up?"

"I really only started to read a few years ago." Pausing, she shook her head as if to brush away an insect. "When I was young, the only thing I liked was sport."

"Do we need to keep standing like this?"

We sat down at my table. I called the waiter, who seemed quite a surreal character. About sixty, with dreadlocks and the vague expression of someone who'd just been smoking something rather stronger than a cigarette. I ordered another white wine for me and a beer for her.

"What sport did you do?"

"I was good at almost everything, but I was best at track and field. I was the fastest person in my school, and that included the boys."

Bob Marley arrived with the wine, the beer and a slice of toast cut into quarters.

"I'd have been happy not to have been the slowest in my class."

She looked over at me as if to check if I was serious.

"All right, I'm exaggerating," I said. "I wasn't the slowest in the class, but I wasn't one of the best at sports. I tried lots of them, but wasn't good at any of them. The funny thing is that for years I dreamt of becoming a champion at something. What about you?"

"I was an athlete. From the end of school up until the age of twenty-five, I was a professional athlete. I ran the 100 and the 200 metres. What are you involved in?"

What a strange question, I thought. *What are you involved in?* What does it mean, to be involved in something? Being involved means dedicating yourself, being alert, showing an interest, taking care, bothering. I don't really know what I'm *involved* in, I thought with a touch of alarm.

"I write novels. I did other things before, but I gave them all up a few years ago. Now I just write."

"So you're a writer?" she said, genuinely surprised.

"Yes."

"What's your name?"

I told her my name. She didn't recognise it. She was sorry, she added.

"It's the first time in my life I've met a writer. What kind of novels do you write?"

I emptied my glass and signalled to Bob Marley to bring me another. It was my fourth – in other words, I'd had more or less a full bottle. I'd been drinking too much in the last few months. That wasn't a good thing, but I didn't want to think about it.

"What kind of novels do I write? A few years ago I'd

have been able to answer that question easily. Now I don't know."

"What do you mean?"

"A few years ago I liked what I wrote. Now I'm not sure that as a reader I'd like to read books like mine. That's why I find it hard to say what kind of novels I write. It must be some kind of avoidance syndrome, which is something I'm quite good at. Avoidance, I mean."

She half closed her eyes, as if making an effort to grab hold of a rebellious idea. "Why are you spending your time chatting with me? You don't give me the impression that you're trying to pick me up."

"Be careful when you talk to writers. They're listening to you, but what they're really thinking about is how they can use the conversation in their next book."

"Do you mean that *you're* thinking about how to use this conversation in your next book?"

"To tell the truth, what we're saying to each other doesn't have much to do with the subject of my new book, which is only at the idea stage anyway. But you never know." Then, after a brief pause: "And you don't give me the impression you're trying to pick me up either."

A slight smile, tinged with irony, hovered over her lips.

"What's the book about?"

"That's a good question. The problem is that you often

don't really know what your novel's about until you've written it. But basically, it's a story about a woman leading a normal life – whatever that means: *a normal life* – a straight woman who one fine day falls in love with a girl."

It was as if she had seen a ghost. She looked at me as if she had suddenly lost her balance or her sense of direction. I was about to ask if she was all right, if something was wrong, when she gestured with her hand.

"I have to go. I'm late for work."

Work, at this hour? What kind of work begins after 8.00 in the evening? Night clerk, taxi driver, policewoman, pharmacist, porter at a fruit market, nurse, barmaid, radio presenter, garbage collector, prostitute?

"Maybe I'll see you around."

She studied my face for a few more seconds. Then she stood up and left the café.

By the time I got to the Caffè del Pescatore the following day, the sun had already gone down. She was sitting at her table, a half-empty mug of beer in front of her, her spiral notebook open, a few pencils scattered around. She looked as if she had been there for a while.

"Good evening," I said.

She looked up, but didn't seem to recognise me. It was a prolonged and somewhat embarrassing gaze.

I was just about to remind her that we had met the previous evening, that we had chatted, that I was a decent guy, stuff like that, when she said, "Do you know me?"

"Do I know you? You mean from before yesterday?"

She regarded me for a long time, apparently searching my face for clues to a plot, a strategy. She seemed to be looking for a hidden meaning. At last she appeared to relax.

"I'm sorry. It's just that . . . It's what you said yesterday."

"What did I say yesterday?"

"You talked about your new novel."

"Is it such a terrible idea?"

She gave a hint of a smile.

"Would you like to sit down?"

I sat down and signalled to the Rastafarian. He nodded knowingly and, a minute later, arrived with a glass of wine and two small bowls of olives and *taralli*. Actually I'd have liked to order a beer, but Bob Marley seemed so pleased with himself – a professional doing his job properly – that I didn't have the heart to send the wine back.

"So, what's wrong with my novel, or rather, to be precise: with my *idea* for a novel?"

She shrugged. It was clear that, for the moment at least, my question wouldn't be answered. So I decided to change the subject.

"When you left yesterday, you said you were late for work."

"I keep an old couple company at night. I sleep at their

place, and the next morning a Georgian carer takes over from me. Actually they can look after themselves, but they pay me to sleep there. It makes them feel safe. But I do other jobs too." The last words had the vague tone of self-justification.

If there's a stereotype for a care worker, she was the exact opposite. That unexpected answer of hers jarred and made me uneasy. Like a leak, a bad smell, a dissonant chord. A dream you have with your eyes open, the disturbing kind that straddles the thin line between waking and sleep.

A crack in the wall.

"Why did you ask me if I knew you?"

"A few years ago my face was in the newspapers quite a lot."

I shook my head. I didn't remember anything and, although I find it strange when I think back on it now, it didn't occur to me to ask her why her face had been in the papers. She finished her beer – it's got warm, I thought – and started putting her things back in her bag. I played with a *tarallo*, popped it into my mouth whole, felt the surface crisp with oil yielding beneath my teeth, and drained my own glass. I didn't know what to say, but would have liked her not to leave. She spoke when she was already on her feet, pulling me up short.

"What's the problem with your books?"

I rubbed my face, to gain time, I suppose.

"I'd need somebody to tell me. It's something to do with truth – or the lack of it."

"Aren't you happy?"

"I'm afraid not."

She nodded, as if my answer had satisfied her.

"Can I ask you something?"

"Yes."

"What do you write in that notebook? Or draw? I've been wondering since yesterday."

"Lists."

"Lists? What do you mean?"

"I'll tell you next time we meet." Waving goodbye, she stood up and left.

I sat there for another ten minutes or so, but didn't even open my laptop. I was sure I wouldn't write a line.

By now the Rasta was greeting me as if we were old friends. He gave me a knowing smile and asked – but it wasn't a question – if I wanted the *usual*. I said yes, and he nodded and walked away.

"Signora Sara hasn't arrived yet," he said, bringing me the tray with the wine, *taralli* and olives. "But she'll come," he added. "She almost always does."

Signora Sara. A strange way to put it, I thought. A bizarre mixture of familiarity and respect. Why did he call her that?

I looked around me. Opposite my table, at the end of the awning-covered terrace, were a concrete breakwater and then the sea. The words *concrete structure* came into my mind. *Concrete*

Structure and Sea at Sunset was the title of the composition. In itself the concrete would have been quite ugly, but, associated in that way with the sea and the late afternoon sky, it had an austere beauty. The tens, the hundreds of bits of gravel sticking out by a few millimetres from the surfaces of the concrete blocks evoked a hidden life imprisoned in the inert material. In the distance there were a few fishing boats, and, once you stopped thinking about yourself, you could even smell the sea.

"Good evening," Sara said.

"Good evening."

"You're early today."

The waiter materialised, and for a few moments I had the distinct impression that the two of them were in cahoots and that I was involved in a game the meaning of which escaped me.

"Hello, Cosimo. I'll have some wine today too. And something to eat. I haven't eaten a thing since this morning."

Cosimo – now I knew both their names – nodded like Mr Wolf in *Pulp Fiction*.

My name's Cosimo, I solve problems.

He came back with a bottle of wine in a bucket – *Since you're both drinking, I'm not going to keep coming back and forth* – then with a tray of small pieces of *focaccia*, mozzarella balls, and diced *prosciutto crudo* cut into small cubes.

"Yesterday, you mentioned truth. What did you mean?"

"It's quite hard to talk about . . ."

"Well, why don't you try and I'll try to understand. If anything's beyond me, you can explain it again, or maybe draw a diagram."

"I didn't mean—"

"I know. I'm sorry. I still find it hard to hold back on the cutting remarks, although I've been working on it for years."

"Do you have a cigarette?" I said, without much hope.

She shook her head with a hint of regret. "I haven't smoked in ages."

I nodded gravely, as if an important preliminary point had been clarified and the moment had come to touch on more fundamental questions.

"Well?" she insisted.

"I have the impression that I always just skim the surface, that I never manage to delve deeper. That's not the best way to tell the truth. It was different at the beginning, but there you are."

She regarded me silently, waiting.

"Let's put it this way: I use too many fade-outs."

"How do you mean?"

"Like in films. A fade-out is when an image grows darker until it's replaced by a black screen. It means that one scene has come to a peaceful end, and you can move calmly on to the next one. By using a fade-out, you can avoid having to talk about what you don't like, what doesn't feel right, what's disagreeable, for us or for other people."

"And you use fade-outs?"

"More than I should, I'm afraid. When I get to those points, I fade out and start again with another scene. What I should really be writing about is what happens when the fade-out starts. What's behind the fade-out. That's where the truth is, but I have problems going there."

"Those are danger zones."

"Precisely. You know about danger zones?"

"Quite a lot."

We were silent for a few minutes and I was surprised not to feel uncomfortable.

"Would you like to hear a story?"

"Yes."

"I told you I liked sports, and ran very fast. After I'd finished school I joined the police sports team."

"Didn't you go to university?"

"Yes, I did. I studied Law. That was the agreement I'd made with my father. *You can carry on with sport only if you promise me that you'll continue your studies.* I can still hear him in my head. I mean, I can actually hear my father's voice, as if he were here, but in another room."

"Your father . . ."

"Was a judge. He's dead now. He died three years ago." She half closed her eyes and it seemed almost as if she were trying to hear that voice from another room. "Anyway, I kept my promise. That one, at least. I graduated the same year I won a medal for the last time in an Italian championship. Bronze. If you're used to more valuable metals, a bronze means various things. Among them being: It might be good to think about quitting. So I quit before I found myself lagging behind girls who were younger, stronger and more talented. Then I did the course to become a police officer, took the exam, passed it, and went from being a member of the sports team to a deputy commissioner on probation. I'd liked the police since I was a little girl, I was fascinated by T.V. series featuring policewomen, and if I was asked what I wanted to be when I grew up I'd say, 'I want to be a policewoman.' My father would have liked me to be a lawyer like him, but I didn't even sit the exam."

"You haven't said anything about your mother."

"She died when I was very young. I don't remember her face or even her voice. All I remember is the smell of milk and biscuits."

I took the wine bottle from the bucket and filled our glasses.

"After the course, and after a year spent teaching in a police school – which bored me to tears – I found myself, at my own request, in charge of the robbery squad in a big city police department. They put me there because nobody else wanted to do it, it clearly worried them."

"Because it isn't a job for women?"

"Precisely. The idea is that even the head of the squad goes out on the streets. But nobody expected a female head to do that."

"So what did you do?"

"I spent a few days learning the ropes, and then I told the elderly inspector, the one who stayed in the office and determined the rota, that the following week I'd go out on a motorbike with the others. He gave me a strange look. I asked him if there was a problem and he said no, of course there were no problems. He chose one of the oldest officers to ride the bike. Or at least, someone who seemed very old to me at the time. He was forty-five, I remember; it was one of the first things he told me. Forty-five doesn't seem that old to me now. Anyway, Lotar – that was his name – was a giant, an ex-wrestler, completely bald, with really scary green eyes. He'd been with the police for twenty-five years and had always done that same job, going out on a motorbike, I mean, and chasing criminals. At that age you usually moved on to easier assignments, but he liked the street and had always refused to be transferred to another squad. God knows what's become of him. He must be retired by now . . ."

I realised that the sky had changed colour and the sea had turned deep blue. The wind had risen, and there was a sense of menace and excitement in the air, the kind you sometimes feel in times of transition. The waiter was nowhere to be seen, there were no other customers, and everything suddenly gave off the feeling that something tragic was about to happen. I shivered, just once.

"Lotar made an effort to treat me normally, but he was

embarrassed. He'd never had a woman as a partner, let alone a woman who was his chief. He drove very carefully, took me around bars, leisure centres, amusement arcades – the places where you encountered known criminals. He knew them all and they all knew him. He pointed them out and told me their names, their nicknames, their specialities. Burglary, pick-pocketing, bag-snatching, drug dealing, robbery, moneylending, receiving stolen goods. A tour of Crime City. Then, just as we'd decided to go for a coffee and a quick smoke, we heard someone shouting behind us. Lotar turned the bike around, using a manoeuvre I'd never seen before; I remember the sound of the tyres on the asphalt and the terrified face of a woman who was starting to cross the road and almost had to jump to get back onto the pavement. We were just in time to see a moped with two young men on it racing away down the wrong side of the street, weaving in and out among the cars, and a woman trying to get up off the ground. Lotar hesitated for a second because I was with him – though I may only have imagined it – and set off after them. It was a crazy chase, still on the wrong side of the road, with tyres screeching and car horns blaring and people screaming. We caught up with them after a few blocks. Lotar hemmed them in against the kerb and they both fell off their bike. The one who was driving must have hurt himself because he remained on the ground, but the other one ran off. From that point on, my memory is unclear. Everything disappears other than me and the escaping man.

There's no sound. I jump off the bike and run after him. I'm on good form, I run very well, very cleanly, one foot after the other, like in a race you know you can win."

A slight smile appeared on her lips, as if she were talking about a love affair, a first kiss, not about following a bag-snatcher.

"Did you catch him?"

"It was as if he was moving in slow motion. I caught up with him without any effort and gave him a shove. He lost his balance and fell, and I jumped on him and started punching and slapping his head."

"Didn't he react?"

"You know, I can't remember. I'm sure he didn't hit me. Maybe he tried to react, or to struggle free, but then Lotar arrived. He knew him. All he said was, 'Stay where you are,' and the guy froze. I managed to get some handcuffs on him. Then I stood up. Lotar and I looked at each other for a few seconds, maybe longer; I'll never forget that look he gave me. In the end all he could say was, 'You run very fast.'"

She gazed into the distance. Beyond me, beyond the bar counter, beyond the street outside. All the way to the lost domain of that perfect gesture, and all the other perfect gestures, and her youth, invincible, universal and lost, as it is for everybody. There was a kind of giddy expression in her eyes that forced me to look away.

When she came back to her senses, she said that she'd lost

her train of thought, it was late, she had to go. It was nice talking to you, I must go now, we can meet tomorrow if you like,
yes, I'd like that, maybe . . . Maybe what? Nothing, just maybe.
Good evening, goodnight.

　　Goodnight.

I arrived earlier than I had before. I would never have admitted
it, but I was early because I wanted more time to chat with her.
It was a cloudy afternoon and the air was cool. Temperature
below the seasonal average, Atlantic disturbance on the way, a
foretaste of autumn. All the colours were faded; there was a
strong smell of salt and seaweed; the waves lashed the concrete
breakwater, sending up little spurts of foam. This time, the café
was less deserted than usual. One of the tables was occupied by
four muscular young men who, if you trusted the stereotype,
looked like smugglers taking a coffee break.

　　I sat down and put my laptop on the table, but didn't even
switch it on. I sat there looking at the sea and the foam, and
listening to the harmonious, rhythmical cacophony of the
smugglers' conversation. Not so much the conversation, more
the sounds of their voices. Cosimo waited for about ten minutes before appearing with a glass of wine, little portions of
panzerotto and bruschetta, and roasted almonds.

　　"Are you waiting for Signora Sara?"

　　I was about to say no, I came here to write, can't you see
the laptop? Instead of which, I said yes.

"She doesn't usually come on Thursdays."

"When we said goodbye yesterday, she told me she'd be here today."

"Then she will be." He hesitated for a few moments, slightly bewildered, then added, "It means she's coming specially."

I didn't know how to answer that. We held each other's eyes for a few seconds.

"She doesn't usually confide in people," he said.

"Ah . . ."

"Why are you here?"

"What do you mean?"

"You aren't a journalist, are you?"

"No."

"Good," he said, and walked away.

At least half an hour went by, the other customers – including the smugglers – left, and I was alone while the black and white of the landscape became ever more black and white, with all the shades of grey in between. I started to feel nervous, then ridiculous and finally sad, and decided to leave. I'd turned in my seat to call my Rasta friend and ask for the bill when she appeared on the terrace.

She was carrying a gym bag over her shoulder, and as she came closer I smelled shampoo and soap. Through her tight-fitting jeans you could sense her muscular legs.

"How are you? Have you been here long?"

I couldn't restrain a slightly – absurdly – resentful tone.

"Actually I've been here for three quarters of an hour. I was just about to go."

"Don't go. I came specially to talk to you. I don't usually come here on Thursdays."

"Yes, that's what the Rasta – I mean Cosimo – said."

"What did you call him?" she asked with a laugh.

"Well, with those dreadlocks . . ."

She smiled briefly, looking in the direction of the counter.

"I really like talking to you," she said without warning.

That took me by surprise. I didn't know what to say; I have problems with compliments. So I gave her a smile that probably looked like a grimace and, in order to overcome my embarrassment, said the first thing that crossed my mind.

"I wonder how old Cosimo is."

"Fifty-eight next month, on the 21st to be precise," she replied in a strangely neutral tone, surprising me again. I'd only said that to have something to say, to fill a gap, not because I was really interested in how old Cosimo was. But now I felt like asking how come she knew the strange waiter's birthday, and what the nature of their relationship was. Only I really couldn't ask that. In some vague way, I felt that now was not the moment.

"You told me you'd explain about the lists," I said, trying to regain control of the conversation. Cosimo arrived with a glass of wine for Sara.

"The lists. You're right." She half closed her eyes as if making an effort to put her tangled thoughts into some kind of order.

"I had a friend . . . a philosophy teacher."

"At university?"

"No, in a school. We were seeing each other for a while. A pity; I wasn't ready for a relationship . . ." She broke off with a gesture of annoyance. "Why do I keep telling pointless lies?"

"What lies?"

"We say we aren't ready for a relationship, we aren't ready to commit, when in fact we don't like someone enough, or don't like them at all. It's a way of justifying ourselves, not admitting our own responsibility, not recognising that we've taken advantage of someone else."

"Did you take advantage of your friend?"

"I don't know."

She seemed to want to add something. Instead, she said nothing, but ran her thumb over her glass, back and forth, up and down, as if to check that it was really smooth, that there weren't any unexpected irregularities or rough edges. There was something desperate, something almost unbearable, in that repeated meaningless gesture. When she stopped, I felt an absurd sense of relief.

"I told my friend – his name's Massimo – that I wanted to write my memories down in the form of a story, a kind of memoir. Not because I have any desire to publish it. I wanted to write because I had the sensation that everything was escaping from my hands. For months and months I was obsessed by the thought that I might forget everything. Massimo told me he didn't think it was a good idea."

"Why?"

"He said memoirs and diaries are tiresome to write and painful to reread. You start out full of enthusiasm, and then, unless it's an exceptional case, you stop after a few days or weeks. And when you reread what you've written, you almost always feel a sensation of strangeness. And often a kind of embarrassment too. But he also said that writing down your memories was an excellent idea, because there are lots of things that, if you lose them, you never find again."

"And so?"

"And so he said that the best way to collect your memories, to not let them become scattered, was to make lists. Every list should have a title, something like: *Titles of the songs we danced to at school parties* or *Childhood sweets*. Every item on the list should be just a few words. If they were only one word, better still."

"Your friend must have been a fan of Perec."

"Perec, that's right. He mentioned him, suggested I read a book of his – I can't remember the title, it was something to do with memory and lists – but I've never found it in any bookshop."

"*Je me souviens.*"

"I'm sorry?"

"That's the title of that book by Perec. *Je me souviens* – *I Remember*. I read it in Paris many years ago. You're right, it's impossible to find, the Italian translation anyway. Can you read French?"

"No. I speak English and I can get by in Spanish."

"*Childhood sweets* is interesting," I said after a pause.

"I actually wrote it the day we first met. Do you want to hear it?"

I did. So she bent over her bag, searched for a few seconds and then brought out the spiral notebook.

"Let's see, ahhh, here it is. 'Elah sweets, Rossana sweets, rolls of liquorice (bought loose from the kiosk in the park), potato cakes (from Nonna Rosa's pastry shop), brioche, Urrà Saiwa wafers, Nutella, Duplo chocolate bars, currant buns (from the student bakery), little pieces of quince jelly wrapped in cellophane (also from the kiosk in the park), apricot-flavoured Kinder Brioss, Togo biscuits'."

She stopped reading and looked over at me.

"How about the slices of brioche loaf at children's parties?" I said. "I don't know if you had them at your parties or your friends' parties."

"Of course we had them. But that isn't a sweet. If we wanted to add it, we'd have to change the title of the list."

"You're right. It's just that your list reminded me of lots

of things, and one of them was brioche loaf. I forgot that the
list's title was what it was. Maybe we could add Mars and
Smarties, though?"

"Mars and Smarties. Right." Saying this, she wrote something – "Mars" and "Smarties", I assume – in her notebook.

At that moment a ray of sunlight burst through a little gap
in the compact mass of white clouds, as if someone were shining a reflector through them, aimed at the sea and a couple of
fishing boats swaying in the distance.

"How do you choose the subjects for your lists?"

"I don't know. At first, when I started, I followed a few
rules. Most of them were to do with the past. I had titles like
*Unrealised dreams, Films seen during my last year of school, Pieces of
music I listened to when I was at the academy* – the police academy,
I mean. Then I started being a bit freer, and now I let myself be
inspired by whatever comes into my head. A few days ago, for
instance, I got into a lift and there was a smell – the smell of a
person – that was quite unpleasant. Actually it was a real stink;
the air was almost unbreathable. So I thought of making a list of
smells I don't like, and then another list of smells I do like. And
I realised a whole lot of things while I was writing those lists."

The ray of sunlight still illumined the sea, even though the
boats were moving away.

"What became of Massimo?"

"I don't know."

"Why do you come here to the bar to write your lists?"

"I can't do it at home. When it's too quiet, I become aware of the solitude and I can't concentrate. I can do it sometimes in the evening, with the television on, but mostly I need there to be other people around – or at least to hear voices – and I'm fond of this place."

"Are you sure that the lists are more effective than a diary? I mean as . . . let's say as a therapeutic tool."

"That's the question I asked Massimo, in almost the same words."

"And what did he reply?"

"Could you tell me the films you liked the most – let's say five of them – in your first year at university?"

"I'm sorry?"

"That's the question Massimo asked me. Can you answer that question?"

"No, how can I remember?"

"And what effect does it have on you, not remembering?"

I concentrated for about twenty or thirty seconds, then shook my head, feeling ill at ease.

"Well?"

"I start to feel panic."

"That's it exactly. I lived in a state of panic. I mean, it wasn't intense panic, but it was constant."

"And now?"

"Now it's better, for many reasons. The lists have certainly helped."

The ray of sunlight had been swallowed up again by the clouds. Sara took a sip of wine and called the waiter over.

"You still smoke, Cosimo, don't you?"

"Of course I smoke. I started at the age of twelve; I'll stop when I die."

"Could you let us have a couple of cigarettes?"

"Do you still smoke, Signora?"

"Every now and again."

"Well, I have these, I don't know if you like them," Cosimo said, taking out a crumpled packet of yellow MS. Sara said they'd be fine, he handed two of them to us, and we lit them. I wondered how long it had been since I had last smoked a cigarette. At first I'd counted the months and even the days since I'd quit, but then I'd forgotten to keep count.

Cosimo's MS was rough and strong and went to my head. Sara held her cigarette between her thumb and index finger. She seemed to be smoking carefully, as if she didn't want to waste a single shred of the tobacco as it turned to ash. Outside, on the road, a car passed with its windows down and the stereo pouring out Neapolitan songs at full volume.

"Would you like to play a game?" she asked me when the music had faded into the distance.

"What game?" I replied, noticing that I still had half my cigarette left while she was already stubbing hers out in the ashtray.

"Let's make a list together. The films you saw in your first year at university."

I said I didn't think I could.

"Come on, let's try," she insisted, suddenly familiar, as if the moment had come to drop any pretence of formality. "What year are we talking about?"

"1986–87," I replied after a brief hesitation.

"Do you have any memory that connects your first year at university to a particular film?"

Overcoming the sense of anxiety the task aroused in me, I managed to remember a film. I'd seen it with two old friends one afternoon after a seminar. It was one of those films I considered prophetic, one of those I thought spoke directly to me among all the people in the cinema. The story of a young boy who's particularly good at telling stories, and who later becomes a writer.

"*Stand by Me*," I said hesitantly. But then others flooded into my mind: *Absolute Beginners, Platoon, Hannah and her Sisters, La Famiglia, The Green Ray, Highlander, The Name of the Rose*. For each one, I remembered the time and the cinema where I'd seen it. For three or four of them, the occasion, too, and even – it seemed to me – the people I'd seen them with.

It was a very strange sensation: by the time I'd finished, the panic had disappeared, replaced by a calm I hadn't felt for quite a while – or maybe that I'd never known in that form. Could it really be as simple as that? I mean, could you really regain control of a piece of the past that seemed lost in the whirlpool of memory by writing a simple list? This is quite absurd, I thought, although without conviction.

"It wasn't hard, was it?"

"No, it wasn't hard," I replied slowly.

"I have another one I'd like to read to you."

"Go on."

"It's a list of things I liked most in my life in the police. A coffee at the bar opposite headquarters with the boys from my squad, before starting work in the morning. A coffee at a normal bar, early in the morning, after a night spent working. The night-time operational meeting, when there are arrests to make the next morning. Climbing in between the sheets in the morning after a night spent working, falling asleep straight away and waking up at lunchtime. The smell of the corridors at headquarters. The adrenalin – and also the fear – just before an operation, and touching the grip of your pistol under your jacket and knowing it was there. The coffees and cigarettes during interrogations at night. The times when you entered a bar frequented by known criminals and they realised immediately that you were police."

"Do you miss all those things?"

"Do I miss them? Yes. And no. It isn't as simple as that. And now I have to go and see my old couple. Are you busy tomorrow evening?"

"I haven't been busy for quite a while."

"Shall I see you here, then?"

"Yes."

"All right. Tomorrow's my free evening."

The following day, the rain arrived, with all the determination of those atmospheric phenomena that leave no room for doubt. The end of summer, the beginning of autumn. My car moved forward between drops so big, so thick and fierce, that I couldn't tell them apart on the windscreen wiper. Running the short distance between the car and the entrance to the bar, my trousers got soaked to above the knee. The only tables were under the brick canopy. All the others had been stacked up, and the awning was being shaken by angry gusts of wind. It looked as if it would collapse at any moment. There were no customers, and Cosimo seemed to be there only because he was waiting for Sara and me.

"In my opinion you can sit outside if you wish; the water won't come in. But if you prefer, you can sit inside, near the counter. I'll move a table and two chairs."

"I'm fine outside."

"Would you like a cigarette?"

"Maybe later, thanks," I said, thinking with a touch of shame of my dizziness the day before.

"Then I'll bring you some wine and something to eat. I'm sure the signora will be here soon."

He didn't move, though. He stood there, looking at me.

"Treat her well."

"I'm sorry?"

"Signora Sara."

Once again I didn't know what to say. He let a few seconds pass.

"She arrested me. I was dealing in those days. It was the only time I wasn't beaten up."

I don't know if he was about to add something or had finished, but just then Sara appeared. She too had been caught in the rain and was quite wet.

"Do you think it's raining?" she said with a smile.

Cosimo nodded and walked away, his movements as smooth as those of an English butler – the unlikeliest comparison you could imagine.

He came back a few minutes later and put down the usual tray laden with wine and food.

"So, do you want to hear my story?" Sara asked when we were alone again.

"Yes."

"I was in charge of the robbery squad for almost two years before I was transferred to Narcotics, where there's never any chance you'll be idle. You can arrest all the dealers you want, you can confiscate guns and drugs – there'll always be new dealers and lots more drugs in circulation. There's never any lack of work, and if you're good at it it's a perfect launch pad for a great career in the police."

I was about to say something, but she didn't give me time.

She repeated her last words. The same words, but with a different intonation, an ironic, bitter one. *A great career in the police.*

"An old inspector told me once that of all the officers he'd known, I was the one best suited to that job. He told me he'd never have thought he could say something like that to a woman, but that there was no doubt in his mind at all."

"Why? What did you have that the others didn't?"

"He said I had all the qualities of a male officer, plus I was a woman. And, being a woman, I could go places where a man would never have been able to go."

"Have you ever been married?"

"No. When this thing happened, I'd been with a man for a couple of years. Marcello. I always have to make a bit of an effort to remember his name. He wasn't very different from all the guys I'd been with before."

"In what way?"

"Handsome and a bit stupid." She broke off. "No, that's not quite right. Handsome and not too intelligent. Marcello wasn't stupid. He was a handsome young man, and he was also a good young man; he was a lawyer; he did lots of sports; he wanted to marry me; he said our children would be very beautiful and things like that. Once, only once, when I first knew him, I made the mistake of giving him a book as a present. He thanked me with a very polite smile – he was always very polite – then put the book on a shelf and told me he'd read it soon. The book stayed there like a relic, and I'm sure if we walked into his apartment today, we'd find it in the same place. I know now that the only reason I could stand Marcello was because we didn't see much of each other thanks to my work."

"In other words, it wasn't exactly a love story."

"No, it wasn't. I know it's a horrible thing to say, but he was a useful way of filling my free time and easing the boredom. He was like a light white wine, the kind we're drinking now. It doesn't have much taste, but it's pleasant enough when you drink it cold. Although you have to be careful *how much* you drink of it, because it could give you a headache."

It seemed to me all at once that something was missing. It took me a few seconds to realise that it was the rain. It had stopped, and the almost deafening noise of the raindrops on the awning was gone.

"As I was saying, there's never any lack of work in Narcotics. We mounted lots of operations, arrested lots of people, and the Prosecutor's office trusted us. We arrested gangs of Albanians, Serbs, Turks, Calabrians and Puglians too, obviously."

"I have no idea how an operation like that works. How do you know there's a gang that's dealing drugs, how do you investigate it, what do you do?"

"Almost all drugs investigations, but not only drugs investigations, come about thanks to informants."

"What's the difference between an informer and a witness? If there is one."

"Oh yes, there is. The informant is someone – usually a criminal – who provides information to the police but without making a statement or appearing in court. An informant has to remain anonymous."

"Is it legal? How can anyone defend themself against the statements of an anonymous person?"

"Nobody can be charged, let alone sentenced, on the basis of a statement by an informant. Without a guarantee of anonymity, no criminal would give information to the police, or the *carabinieri*, or the customs authorities. Such information can only be used to launch an investigation or point it in the right direction. It makes it possible to intervene in time when something's about to happen – a robbery, a murder, a drugs delivery – but admissible evidence has to be found in other ways, through phone taps, searches, testimony, surveillance and all the rest. From the legal point of view, anonymous tipsters and informants are worthless, but from an investigative point of view they're essential."

"And why do criminals confide in the police?"

"For many reasons. Because they want to damage or eliminate a rival, because they want to make sure the police will give them an easy time over their own activities, sometimes out of friendship, and often just for the pleasure of accusing someone else."

Cosimo the Rasta arrived with a plate of bruschetta and *panzerotto*. He asked us if we wanted more wine. Then he asked us if we wanted cigarettes, and Sara said thanks, but this time she'd brought her own. Cosimo disappeared and she took out a packet of Marlboros.

"I thought we might want to smoke more than one and that it wouldn't be polite to get through the whole of Cosimo's packet." Then, after a pause: "Cosimo was an informant of mine in his other life." Lighting a cigarette, she smoked nearly half of it without saying anything else. Then: "I don't know why I decided to talk to you."

There was nothing to say to that, so I just shrugged. Nodding, she stubbed her cigarette out in an ashtray. The packet was still on the table, and she pushed it towards me. I shook my head.

"You don't want to smoke," she said to gain time.

"Later. Just one, otherwise I'll start again."

"Knowing how to deal with informants is maybe the most important part of a police officer's job. Maybe also the hardest."

"Why?"

"Because you have to be able to walk a fine line between what's right and what's wrong. You have to take care not to promise anything illegal, or make any promises you can't keep. In practice, that means almost never making any promises at all. You have to be able to distinguish between good information and bullshit, between what the informer has direct knowledge of and what he's heard and what maybe someone has said to him because they know he talks to you and want to give you false information. You have to be aware that some categories of individuals are more dangerous than others, and more likely to provide information that's completely or partly invented."

"For example?"

"For example, heroin addicts. When they're suffering withdrawal symptoms, they're quite capable of telling you they saw the pope committing a robbery and know where he took shelter and who his accomplices were."

"When did you meet Cosimo?"

"Almost immediately after I moved over to Narcotics. We picked him up in possession of a few grams of cocaine. When he was released some months later, he came to see me in my office. He said he'd come to thank me for the way I'd treated him – some of my men had been about to beat him up and I'd told them not to. He said I could ask him for help at any time." She lowered her voice a little, as if it were a conditioned reflex. "He was always straight with me, I never had false information from him, and he never asked for anything in return, except that we shouldn't do anything to his son, who ran an amusement arcade."

"And now is he . . .?"

"Is he still involved in that kind of thing? I don't know. I don't think so, but frankly I'm not really interested."

She lit another cigarette, and as she smoked it her features hardened and the lines on her face took on a different, harsher texture. She started speaking again without looking at me and without moving her head.

"A basic rule is to keep your informants at a distance. You have to establish a rapport, otherwise you won't get anything from them, but you always have to make it clear that you're a copper and they're . . . well, that they're different."

The rain seemed definitely to be over. There were a few gaps in the clouds over the sea, beyond the breakwater. It was turning beautiful and dark at the same time. Cosimo reappeared but didn't come over to us. Walking to the edge between the terrace and the breakwater, he also lit a cigarette. I had the very real impression that he was standing guard.

"When I started to do athletics – I was fourteen – there was a girl who was older than me. She was sixteen, maybe seventeen. She also did the 100 and 200 metres, and the long jump too. She wasn't especially good, but she was beautiful. She looked like that French actress, Carole Bouquet. Whenever our eyes met, I blushed. On the few occasions she actually spoke to me, I'd turn an even deeper red and stammer a reply, dying with shame at the idea that the other girls or the trainer would notice."

What did this story have to do with anything? Why did it make me feel slightly uncomfortable? I was trying to understand when she broke off abruptly, half closed her eyes, touched her forehead with one hand, and pursed her lips. She seemed to be making an effort to remember something.

"I can't remember what her name was. It's absurd, but I can't remember. Anyway, after a year, she stopped coming to training – like I said, she wasn't a great athlete – and I stopped blushing when our eyes met. That was the end of that strange adolescent upset. A shock to my sexual identity, my friend Massimo would have said. It's something I haven't thought about for a long time. I'd forgotten about it, and maybe I'll never remember it again.

"I had my first boyfriend when I was about sixteen, and, since then, apart from very short periods, I've practically never been without one or something like one. Maybe I was in love with a couple of them, or thought I was. Or maybe *infatuation* is a more exact word. But there was never any overwhelming passion and never anyone who departed from that pattern.

"That was how I'd come to be engaged to Marcello, the lawyer. And it was while I was engaged to him that I met Roberta."

"Roberta," I echoed, as if to ask a question without actually asking it. She didn't even notice.

"One of my inspectors had received a tip that this girl was dealing. They'd stopped her, searched her car and found a couple of grams of cocaine. You don't automatically arrest someone for possession if it's that small a quantity. A person might have it for personal use – that was what she said – and anyway it depends a lot on which deputy prosecutor is on duty. Anyway, we had to decide what to do, and I told my men to bring her to my office. It's often in situations like this that you acquire new informants. You have someone whose fate is in the balance and you make it clear to them that you might be lenient, but that they'll have to do something for you in return."

"And were you planning to say that to her?"

"First of all I wanted to see what kind of person she was. You need to look them in the face to see if it makes any sense saying something like that. But the real reason I wanted her brought to my office was because I was curious – usually it was my inspectors who talked to the small-time dealers."

"Why were you curious?"

"Because the boys who'd brought her in said she was very beautiful."

"And was she?"

"She was the most beautiful thing I'd ever seen in my life."

She hesitated for a few moments, as if the sentence hadn't satisfied her, as if even that emphatic statement were insufficient to say what she really wanted to say. She seemed to be on the verge of adding something, to clarify or amplify the idea. In the end, though, she just continued her story.

"I tried to sound as professional as I could. I told her she was in a lot of trouble and that according to the rules we'd have to arrest her. I told her I'd like to help her, but in order to do that I needed her to help me too. I was talking to her, but I couldn't look her in the eye. I felt the same way I had all those years earlier, in the changing room at the athletics track, with that other girl."

"What did she say?"

"She started crying, she begged me to help her. We were sitting facing each other, next to my desk, and I remember the exact moment she took my hands. It was like an electric shock going through me, and I felt an almost irresistible impulse to kiss her. I don't know how I managed to hold myself back."

With the effect of a door suddenly being blown wide open by the wind, I remembered her surprised expression at the end of our first encounter. What a crazy coincidence, I told myself, while our words – the ones I thought I remembered – echoed in my head like a poor-quality recording, full of static and interference.

What's your novel about? It's about a woman leading a normal life, a straight woman who one fine day falls in love with a girl. That's the idea, but you never really know what your novel's about until you've written it.

What a crazy coincidence, I repeated, articulating those words in my head. I would have liked to say something, but there wasn't anything to say that wasn't stupid and banal. And pointless.

Sara cleared her throat, took a sip of wine, took out a cigarette, but didn't light it. There was the sound of a siren in the distance, and I wondered if it was the police or an ambulance. I've never been able to tell the difference, although

someone explained to me once that it's all to do with the dur-
ation of the notes that make up the sound. I was about to ask
Sara, not because I was interested but because the silence was
weighing on me.

When she resumed her story, the tone of her voice had
changed. It was neutral, almost laconic. The story started to
flow with disturbing regularity, as if she were reading a police
report.

She told the girl that she would let her go. She would have
to remand her on bail, she couldn't avoid that, but in her report
she would point out that the cocaine might have been for personal use. When they said goodbye, she gave the girl her mobile
number and told her to call her if she had any information on
the people she'd bought the drugs from.

A few days later, Roberta sent her a message asking if
they could meet without explaining the reason. Lying to herself, telling herself it was work, that Roberta must have some
information to pass on to her, Sara made an appointment to
meet her.

There was no information – nothing significant at least – but
an affair began that would last more than a year. Sara and
Roberta got into the habit of seeing each other almost every
day. Roberta often had cocaine at home, a *lot* of cocaine. Sara
soon stopped asking her – and asking herself – how she got
hold of it and if it really was all for personal use. In fact, after a
bit of resistance, she let herself be persuaded to try it. And then

had to try it again, and then again, until, to cut a long story short, the situation got completely out of hand.

"I was crazy about her. Actually, I was crazy, full stop. I was more than in love, I was obsessed. I thought about her all day long. Whatever I was doing I'd be thinking about when we'd see each other, when we'd go to dinner together and then go home and make love. Once I was on night shift. I'd done some cocaine with Roberta, and when I got to headquarters I was still completely under the influence."

"Didn't you think . . .? Weren't you afraid that someone might . . .?"

"I was the head of Narcotics. I was one of the good guys. If anyone had asked me how come I was seeing a person who'd been found in possession by my very own team, I was ready to say that she was one of my informants, someone I needed to see often for my work. And since the relationship you have with your informants is a confidential relationship – nobody can force you to pass on what they tell you – I felt completely safe. Actually I was like a little child who covers her eyes thinking that if she does, nobody will be able to see her."

Sara took a deep breath. She looked around as if this were the first time she'd been in the café. She passed her hands over her face and then through her hair. She took another deep breath.

"There's a saying I like very much. It goes like this: Don't run faster than your guardian angel can fly."

"That's nice."

"Well, there I was, a little girl running with her eyes covered, running too fast for her guardian angel to keep up with her."

She finally lit the cigarette she'd been holding all this time, took a couple of drags and then stubbed out almost all of it in the ashtray.

"Before that relationship, had you ever had . . .?"

"Relations with women? No, never. Always only with men, always without a great deal of enthusiasm, which I put down to the fact that I'd never met the right person. I guess that was true, in a way. What's certain is that when I met Roberta, and in all the time she and I . . . well, in all that time, I had the feeling that everything had fallen into place. I'd never been so happy in my life. I was drunk with happiness."

We both fell silent. It was dark and the air had become cooler, enough to make you shiver a little. Between the clouds still swollen with rain, you could sense autumn rubbing its bony hands, summoning the cold air and the grey days and the melancholy of regrets, waiting its turn. Cosimo was somewhere, invisible. Maybe we should go and sit inside, I thought. Maybe you should tell me how it's going to end, I thought. She had to tell me, of course, but in reality I already knew, and I didn't want to hear it.

"When the doorbell rang, I looked at my mobile and saw that it was 4.00 in the morning. Roberta hadn't woken up, and

I had to shake her so that she could go to the door, seeing as we were in her flat and I shouldn't have been there. It was a pathetic precaution. The bell rang again, for a long time, and then someone knocked loudly. In that moment, everything became clear, a second before an oddly shrill voice cried out, '*Carabinieri*! Open up!'

"Roberta had cocaine in the flat. There was a lot of it, and it wasn't even hidden. It didn't take them long to find it. Fifty-eight grams, enough for at least a hundred and fifty or two hundred good doses."

Sara lit another cigarette, and now I also took one. We smoked in silence and this time I didn't feel dizzy.

"The arrest warrant mentioned about twenty suspects, including the two of us. Almost all without criminal records and supposedly above suspicion, apart from a couple of professional dealers, who, it turned out, were the ones who supplied Roberta."

"But why were they arresting you too?"

"A police officer who has knowledge of an offence, who is in a position to prevent it, and who does not do so, is as answerable for that offence as if they had committed it themself. Article 40 of the Penal Code. You know what's weird? It was one of the questions they asked me during my oral exam, article 40 of the Penal Code, the obligation to prevent an offence." Her laugher sounded mechanical, like a jack-in-the-box.

"How come you didn't know anything about the operation?"

"Because it was mounted by our competitors, the *carabinieri*. It was only natural that I wouldn't have known about it. What wasn't natural was that the possibility had never even occurred to me."

"Couldn't you have said that you didn't know anything about the drugs? After all, it was Roberta's flat. She might have been keeping you in the dark."

"I had a look at the arrest warrant. There was a lot of evidence from phone taps and bugs. In her car, Roberta had boasted to a friend she occasionally supplied with cocaine that nothing could happen to her because . . . well, because she knew me. They'd bugged her flat too, and, how shall I put this, the conversations they'd overheard left no room for doubt. About anything. I didn't even try to say that I knew nothing about the drugs."

"You said that Roberta supplied this other friend with drugs. You mean . . ."

"That she was dealing, yes. She was on really good terms with some big-time dealers, and every time she went to see them she bought more than she needed for herself and then passed it on to a few of her friends, the ones she trusted. She felt safe. Actually, it was someone she trusted who'd spilled the beans to the *carabinieri*. Talking of informants."

I looked at her and couldn't find the words to ask the question, but it wasn't hard for her to guess what it was.

"I didn't know, but of course I should have realised. If I hadn't been blind with love, it wouldn't have taken me more than a couple of days to figure things out. Maybe it's more exact to say that I knew but pretended not to. I don't know. It doesn't really matter, when you come down to it."

That was something she must have thought about many times, something she'd finally dismissed from her mind.

"What happened next I remember only in fragments. The most humiliating, most distressing fragments. I remember when they put me in the car, they pushed my head down, which was something I'd seen my men do hundreds of times, and I'd done a few times myself. I remember when they photographed me and took my fingerprints, pressing my fingers on the ink pad and then on the record card. I remember the personal search when I entered prison. I remember being interrogated by the deputy prosecutor, someone I'd worked with many times, someone who trusted me so much that he'd let me have the keys to his office. My lawyer had said that it was better for me to claim my right to remain silent until we knew what exactly they had against me. So when the deputy prosecutor asked me if I intended to answer his questions, I said no. He looked at me and seemed sorry, terribly sorry, about everything. At that moment, for no particular reason, the thought uppermost in my mind was that my relationship with Roberta was over. Since I knew I was about to start crying, and I didn't want to do it in front of them – the prosecutor, his secretary, the *carabinieri*, my lawyer, everyone – I asked to be taken out. I asked, and it seemed like an arrogant gesture on my part, and maybe in a way it was. They took me away and I cried in my cell, and after that everything is swallowed up in a mass of events I can't even remember in chronological order. Life in prison, the transfers to the courtroom for the preliminary hearing, the plea bargaining, the periods of house arrest, the frightened look on my father's face (judges and police officers are the people who are most afraid of the law) the first time he came to the interviews, and then afterwards, that same frightened look, the look of a defenceless old man who was trying to summon up his strength but couldn't. He retired because he couldn't bear going to the courthouse and being with his colleagues, presiding over sessions of the appeals court, sentencing or acquitting, or anything about being a judge, while his daughter – his only daughter, his pride and joy, his reason for living – was in prison. He couldn't die yet; he had to wait for it all to be over. For me to leave prison, for me to be released from house arrest. He waited for my sentence to be confirmed and for my lawyer to get me probation with community service, which meant I wouldn't have to go back to prison. Only then did he give himself permission to die."

We smoked some more and drank some more wine; by this

point it seemed only right to exaggerate both, while the darkness advanced and customers came into the bar from time to time, had a drink at the counter and left, without sitting down, leaving us alone in that tremulous air, watched over by Cosimo the Rasta.

"And how are things now?"

"My life? Not bad, all things considered. I have various jobs, as I said. Sometimes I even get a few assignments from a private detective agency. Mostly anti-drug surveillance of minors."

"What does that mean?"

"If parents are afraid their son or daughter is getting involved in drugs – and they can afford to pay – they go to a private detective agency and ask to have their child put under surveillance. That means following them, checking out the people they meet, the places they hang out and so on. I don't mind it, I know how to do it, and it seems quite useful. I live in a two-room flat, my rent is 300 euros, it's in a block of flats where you always smell stewed turnips on the stairs, but like I said, all things considered, it's not bad."

"What became of Roberta?"

"You won't believe this, but when she got out, she met a man, they got married, and now they have a little girl. Once – just once – I couldn't help myself and went and hung around near the girl's kindergarten. We'd said all kinds of bullshit when we were together, among other things that we'd adopt a little girl, we'd go and live in a country where two women – or two men – could do that. I saw Roberta, but I was some distance away and couldn't tell whether she'd changed, if she had changed at all. A little girl went up to her, she took her by the hand – I noticed she didn't give her a kiss – and they left. Afterwards, when they were gone, I had the impression that I'd dreamt the whole scene, that it hadn't really happened. That *nothing* had really happened. Can you understand that?"

"Yes."

"I've occasionally had the same feeling since. For no apparent reason and without warning. And when I do, I get the idea I'm going mad. That isn't a figure of speech: I really feel as if I'm losing contact with everything, as if I'm going down a road and there's no turning back."

"But then it passes," I said, searching for the right tone.

She looked at me without saying anything. An unexpectedly fearful expression had appeared on her face. I never know how to behave, but at that moment taking her hand came naturally to me.

"Everything passes," I said.

My voice faded slowly on the air while Sara squeezed my hand tightly, as if she was afraid that I might go away.

The White Powder Dance

GIANCARLO DE CATALDO

Translated by Alan Thawley

1

Suite

Two armoured Land Rover Defender 4x4s proceeded in convoy along one of the many tracks running beside the Apurímac River.

The first vehicle, driven by a taciturn *indio*, carried three men.

Next to the driver sat Fernando "Rubio" Rivera, a stocky Mexican with blond hair and oriental-looking cheekbones. No-one had ever seen him without his red-framed, mirrored sunglasses. Some said he used them to hide a scar that not even the most sophisticated plastic surgery could remove. Others put it down to a degenerative disease of the cornea. The truth was that El Rubio only favoured a chosen few with his snakelike gaze: his equals within the cartel, the women he desired and the men he killed. El Rubio was the Sinaloa cartel's Minister of Foreign Affairs.

He was the power behind the plantation.

The second man was a Peruvian named Jaime Gonzales. He was paid by the cartel to supervise cultivation and harvest, handsomely paid in fact, but ultimately he was no more than a mid-ranking employee.

The third man was Tano Raschillà. The sallow, bespectacled young banker managed to look distinguished despite his heavy boots and camouflage gear. He had graduated with flying colours from Bocconi University in Milan before earning a Masters from the London School of Economics. Don Achille Patriarca had decided to invest in this boy from poor peasant stock – his family had always been upstanding and obedient, never dis-loyal – because he was convinced that Tano was someone who would make his way in the world. He was not yet a man of honour, and perhaps he never would be. But Don Achille trusted Tano. That was why he had sent him here, to the V.R.A.E. region of Peru, with an offer that El Rubio would be unable to refuse.

Crowded into the second vehicle were seven Shining Path insurgents, who were responsible for plantation security and whose job it was to ensure that no harm would come to the distinguished visitors. There was also a Mexican with a pock-marked face and inscrutable expression, who was clutching a mariachi guitar. He went by the name of El Norte, and his origins were a mystery to everyone. One thing was certain, though: there was not a more talented *narcocorridos* singer in the whole of Sinaloa. El Norte had been bought by El Rubio to ensure that his feats, and his feats alone, would be celebrated by the singer.

So far they had been on the road for more than an hour. In excellent Spanish, the Italian asked what else there was to see.

"We have another hour or so to go," Jaime Gonzales said. "This is where the new plantings start. You might like to see the channels I had the men dig to regulate the irrigation flow when the seasonal rains are too heavy . . ."

El Rubio and the Italian exchanged eloquent glances. Then El Rubio tapped the driver on the shoulder and signalled him to head back to base camp. Gonzales swallowed his protest.

El Rubio disliked being contradicted. The Mexicans disliked being contradicted. The Mexicans were the bosses.

Thanks to the eclipse of the Colombian cartels and the War on Drugs waged by Bush Sr and Jr, in recent years the Mexican Mafia had taken control. Coca plants were still being grown in the same places – Colombia, Bolivia and Peru – but the producers had been cut out of sales. Gonzales had no love for the Mexicans and was nostalgic for the good old days. The Colombians had never been nice, but the Mexicans were out-and-out bastards. They operated a merciless dictatorship. Terror was their single method of control. Gonzales suspected that they enjoyed the violence they dished out. Dictators and sadists to boot.

The vehicles turned around and headed for base camp.

Watched by armed overseers, the *campesinos* were slowly picking their way in an age-old fashion through the sea of bright green leaves dotted with the crimson flashes of mature berries.

Only one head looked up as the 4x4s drove past.

It belonged to a fifteen-year-old boy with long black hair and soulful eyes turned suspicious by hunger.

His name was Felipe. The previous evening, his Uncle Jorge had turned up at the shack that he shared with his mother and seven brothers and sisters. Embracing Felipe, his uncle announced that they needed men for the harvest.

"Felipe's still a boy," his mother had protested.

"Let me take him in hand, Lupe. We'll soon make a man of him."

"No. He's doing well at school. He needs to carry on."

"Do you have money for his books, sister?"

"I'll find the money somehow."

"You won't, and you know it. There are no alternatives. Off to bed, young man. I'll pick you up at dawn."

Now Felipe was a harvester, working side by side with his uncle. He was learning the secrets of the trade: how to pick off the leaves without damaging the stem while trying to ignore the burning in his chapped fingers.

For a second, Felipe looked straight at the man in the mirrored sunglasses. He had the feeling that El Rubio was looking straight back at him, and shuddered in spite of himself.

"Who are those men, Uncle?"

"Back to work," his uncle hissed nervously. "Keep your head down and don't look. Whatever you do, don't show any curiosity. No-one's allowed to be curious here."

Reluctantly, the boy obeyed. His uncle let a few minutes pass before speaking again, this time with affection.

"I know you're tired. It's hard the first few times, but that'll pass. When you really can't carry on, chew one of the leaves."

"We're allowed to do that, are we? What are we, then, slaves?" the boy said angrily.

"We have been for thousands of years, Felipe. It's our destiny."

"And no-one has ever fought back?"

"Fighting back will just put you in an early grave. Here, take this. It'll make you feel better."

The boy thought about it for a minute, then took the leaf, put it in his mouth and started to chew. The taste was bitter. But he knew he would come to like it. He decided that Uncle Jorge was right. There was no point in fighting. That wasn't the answer. Driving one of those four-wheel-drive monsters. Owning it. Perhaps one day owning a plantation.

That was the answer.

They were greeted at base camp by shouts and bursts of machine-gun fire. El Rubio was first to get out of the Defender. With the others following, he headed towards the small group of guerrillas huddled in the middle of a large, flat expanse of dirt.

"*Que pasa?*"

The shouting subsided. A man in camouflaged overalls with a bandage over his left eye stepped forward.

"Comandante Gualtiero," he said, introducing himself with something like a military salute. "We've captured a spy."

Two boys flung a middle-aged man at El Rubio's feet. His face was a mask of blood and mucous, and his white shirt was in shreds.

"He's the teacher from Cuazcò," someone said.

"The village ten kilometres from here," Jaime Gonzales added.

Bending over the man, El Rubio grabbed him by the hair.

"Are you a spy?"

The teacher started to sob; it was all a misunderstanding. He'd never poked his nose into anything. All he cared about was the kids he taught to read and to count. The guerrillas had made a mistake. He was just a poor wretch.

El Rubio let go of the man's hair. Whether he was a spy or not was irrelevant.

"Take him away," he said. "We need to talk business."

The fighters took hold of the teacher, who let out a blood-curdling cry and started to struggle.

"Away, I said!" El Rubio repeated, starting to get annoyed.

Calm was restored. Jaime Gonzales suggested that they go to his hut, which was the most comfortable one in the camp. El Rubio shook his head.

"It's a nice day. We'll stay outside."

"Forgive me for insisting, Rubio, but I have comfortable chairs and a nice table in my hut, the computer, the best tequila, and . . ."

"You've convinced me," El Rubio smiled.

"Shall we go, then?"

"No. Bring everything out here."

It was a good half hour before the Mexican was happy with the arrangements. All the while, Tano Raschillà kept himself apart from the group, watching the procession of *campesinos* delivering the harvest to the vast warehouses. Tonnes of raw material. Tano ventured an initial estimate. Even taking into account the fact that the product still needed to be refined, the way the market was going and any potential losses, the harvest would still be worth around 1.2 billion euros. From that you had to deduct 10 or 12 per cent for intermediaries, incidental expenses, possible legal fees. So call it a straight billion. If the Mexicans really could deliver three harvests a year, there were colossal amounts of money to be made.

Finally, everything was ready. Two chairs were placed on either side of a functional 'Casus' table in the shade of a giant cedar. Ikea, Tano thought, pitying the Mexican's lack of sophistication. Dismissing Jaime Gonzales with an imperious wave, El Rubio invited the Italian to sit.

The discussions continued for hours, becoming tense at times. Eventually, an agreement was reached. In exchange for a significant reduction in price, Don Achille's family would commit to buying the year's entire production. The Mexicans would be responsible for the first stage, drying the leaves and turning them into cocaine paste. Then the Patriarca family would take over, dealing with transport into Europe and then refining and selling the product. The Mexicans would be paid by direct transfer into numbered accounts held at the Intertrade Bank's Providenciales subsidiary in the Turks and Caicos Islands.

"So we're agreed, *hombre*?"

Tano cleared his throat.

"Yes, Señor Rubio, but we could go even further if you wish . . ."

Tano's proposal was to hold the funds in the accounts until they were combined with the proceeds from the sale of the final product, which would be paid in by the Patriarca family.

"Let's say another billion," he said. That would mean a couple of billion, thinking conservatively. A decent amount of money.

"And what are we supposed to do with all that money?"

The Calabrian proposed a joint venture: short-term investments in high-risk funds and, alternatively or in parallel, acquisitions of "clean" companies operating in the public-works sector.

El Rubio waited a few seconds before replying.

"So in practice, you'd be our bank . . ."

"Both ours and yours. Risk and capital split fifty-fifty."

"But what's in it for us?"

"You'll have direct access to the European market."

"Europe doesn't mean shit anymore."

"Maybe not, but Europeans like us do. We count for a *lot*, Señor Rubio."

El Rubio lit a Cohiba and poured himself a shot of tequila.

"I need to discuss it with the cartel. I'm not sure they'll agree."

"If you agree, Señor Rubio, there'll be a commission of 300,000 euros in it for you. There's no need for everyone to know; it'll stay between us. I could credit it to the account of your choice in, say, five days from now."

"Five days is an eternity, *amigo*."

"Tomorrow evening, then, when I get back to Mexico City."

El Rubio snorted.

Tano leaned towards him.

"I think we could make it four hundred thousand."

El Rubio smiled and took off his sunglasses.

"Deal."

★

The overseers spread the word at sundown: there would be a big *fiesta* at the camp. Everyone was invited. There would be plenty of beer and tequila, and a consignment of fresh, clean *putas* just in from the state capital. Only a few *campesinos* accepted the invitation. The oldest were too tired. The wisest knew that you could never trust the narcos or the guerrillas.

"I'm going," Felipe said.

"You're coming home with me!" Uncle Jorge snapped.

The boy had been chewing coca non-stop. His heart was racing, his brain was on fire. Leaving the old man behind, he started running towards base camp. Jorge limped after him. This was his nephew. If something happened to him, how would Jorge be able to look the boy's mother in the eye?

At the camp, Tano sat at the table of honour with El Rubio, Jaime Gonzales and Comandante Gualtiero. All of them were drunk. Between the beer and tequila was a small mountain of cocaine. Gualtiero started to sing "*Hasta Siempre, Comandante*".

"Still a believer, then?" El Rubio said sarcastically.

"We'll see when the revolution comes," the guerrilla replied with conviction.

The Mexican stroked the top of the mound of coke, almost caressing it.

"This is the only real revolution, comrade!"

Gualtiero took a hefty snort. El Rubio offered the coke to the Calabrian. Tano frowned.

"A real man sells this shit, he doesn't use it," Don Achille had always said.

That was the rule in the Patriarca family. Wise words.

To hell with the rules! Tano didn't want to offend their new partner.

So he powdered his nose like the others.

Felipe wandered around the camp, dazed by the orgy of sounds, colours, smells and violence that hung in the air among the huts and warehouses. He was freaked out by the drug coursing through his system.

Fear and desire were fighting to control his soul.

"This is it. This is how life should be," he told himself. "And someday . . ."

No-one took any notice. He ventured to the far end of the camp, beyond the huts. A barbed-wire fence and, a long way off, the flickering lights of the village.

Suddenly, he heard a faint moan coming from behind him, to his left. He turned towards the huts. There was something there.

"Finish me off, I beg you!"

He went in the direction of the voice.

It was a man. They had crucified him against the door of the last hut. The stench he gave off was unbearable, but there was still a spark of life in his eyes. Felipe recognised the teacher from the village.

"On the table . . . the knife . . . for the love of God!"

There was a table, and yes, on that rough wooden table there was a knife. A bloodstained knife. Felipe picked it up and went over to the teacher.

"Kill me!"

Felipe raised the knife. He knew what to do. He'd done it before with chickens, goats and lambs. Even a pig once. But this was a man. Perhaps. Part of him said, "Do it because it's right." Another part said, "Do it because it'll feel good."

He brought the blade up to the teacher's throat. Closed his eyes. Sliced.

He heard a strangled wheeze and was hit by a spurt of blood. Opening his eyes, he saw the teacher's head dangling on his chest. Almost detached from the body. He felt fear, and an irrational pride.

Two strong hands grabbed Felipe by the shoulders.

Something slammed against his head.

They took him to the man with the mirrored sunglasses after a savage beating that left him barely able to stand.

"I've seen you before," El Rubio said. "You were working in the fields. Why were you looking at me?"

Felipe tried to focus. His eyes were burning and his body was racked with pain.

"I liked your car," he said.

"Would you like to go for a ride?"

"I want to be like you!"

A murmur passed through the little crowd that had gathered to watch. Anyone else in the boy's position would have started to cry, shout and beg. But he seemed almost to want to challenge El Rubio.

One of the guerrillas raised his machine-gun, eager to smash it into the boy's head. El Rubio stopped him.

"What's your name, boy?"

"Felipe."

"You know you've killed a man?"

"Yes."

"Why?"

"I don't know."

An old man threw himself at El Rubio's feet. His name was Jorge, he said, and he was the boy's uncle. He explained that it was the boy's first day at work and that, to keep his strength up, Jorge had taught him to chew coca. He was only fifteen. He wasn't to blame for what he'd done; it was the cocaine. El Rubio dispatched him with a kick and turned to Tano.

"What do you think I should do?"

"With respect," Tano said firmly, "the decision is yours, Señor Rubio."

El Rubio seemed disappointed. Comandante Gualtiero couldn't understand why they were wasting time. The teacher had been condemned to a slow, agonising death, as a warning to other traitors to the cause. The boy had alleviated his suffering.

The boy was a potential traitor. The boy had to die. El Rubio turned again to Tano.

"With respect, I wasn't happy with your first answer."

Tano stepped forward.

"He's shown courage, at least."

They dragged Felipe to his feet. El Rubio beckoned to him.

"If I ordered you to kill a man, here and now . . . would you do it?"

"Yes."

Another shudder passed through the onlookers. The boy really had guts. Either that or he was on another planet.

"Even if that man was your Uncle Jorge?"

"Yes."

"Get me El Norte!" El Rubio shouted. "Where the hell is El Norte?"

Someone went to find the guitar player. El Norte arrived, out of breath. El Rubio explained the situation and ordered him to compose a *corrido* on the spot.

"And make sure it ends right, music man."

"Ends right?"

"That's what I said."

A hush descended. El Norte understood that the boy's fate hung on his song; El Rubio hadn't yet made up his mind. Perhaps he would like the song, and would let Felipe go. On the other hand, he might kill him with his bare hands. El Norte paused for a moment, then picked up his instrument and improvised:

There once was a man who was weeping on the sierra, and right he was to weep because that man was a traitor. There was a young boy who was running on the sierra, and right he was to run because his heart it was pure. The man and the boy crossed paths and the man said to him, "Put an end to my pain. Take the knife of the sierra and put an end to my pain." The boy took the knife of the sierra, and said, "Yes, I will put an end to your pain." The tale spread fast across the whole land and came to the ears of the great, wise chief. El Rubio summoned the boy and said, "Look up when you see me, look me straight in the eye, look up and answer my question. Would you do it again if I asked you to?" "I would do anything for you, my lord," the boy said. El Rubio laughed and said, "This boy's heart is pure and his balls are like diamonds. From today, he will work for me!"

The last arpeggio drifted into the silent night. El Rubio looked at the singer, then looked at Felipe, nodded slowly and said in a serious voice, "From now on, the boy works for me. Give him a drink and a gun. I need good soldiers up there in Mexico!"

The crowd exploded with enthusiasm. Everyone rushed

to complement El Rubio, praising his generosity. El Rubio handed the singer a roll of banknotes and ordered him to make himself scarce.

Everyone crowded around Felipe, the miraculous survivor. A girl with short black hair offered to teach him the mysteries of love. Comandante Gualtiero was disgusted. Another narco-stunt to add to the record. One day there'd be a reckoning. One day he'd stop playing guard dog to these bastards. One day. The day the revolution came. In the meantime, since an example still had to be made, he put two bullets into Jorge's knee. Let him go and complain to that Mexican cocksucker! Then, sniffing a line of good coke, he finally found peace again.

El Norte waited a week so as not to arouse El Rubio's suspicions, and then disappeared. El Rubio ordered his men to comb the area. It wasn't just a question of doing without his favourite singer. Even though he had cheated his cartel out of a significant sum when he'd agreed the deal with the Calabrians, El Rubio still thought of himself as a man of honour. More than anything else, more even than betrayal, he feared losing face. How dare that musician take off without asking permission! El Rubio only calmed down when the body of a man was discovered in a garage on the outskirts of Guadalajara, burned beyond recognition. Next to it was El Norte's unmistakable guitar. The police decided that he had been robbed and then murdered. Someone had discovered that El Norte hid his money inside the instrument, and had tried to get their hands on it. The smashed-up guitar was proof.

But El Norte wasn't dead. In fact, El Norte wasn't even El Norte. His name was Vincent Hueso. Born in Miami to a second-generation immigrant family, he worked as a special agent for the D.E.A., the American Drug Enforcement Administration. Vincent had infiltrated El Rubio's entourage six months earlier. Six months is an eternity for an undercover operation. Narcos are unstable creatures. From one moment to the next, El Rubio could have decided he'd had enough of El Norte. It would only have taken an unwelcome verse in a song to blow everything sky-high. On top of that, the narcos were insanely vindictive. So when an infiltrator disappeared, he had to disappear for ever. Vincent had arranged everything perfectly. He had found himself a dead body, a poor tramp who had starved to death under a flyover, then disfigured and set fire to the corpse to fake his own death.

Vincent reported the location of the plantation and base camp to his bosses, from whom he received an enthusiastic response.

He also wrote to Federico, an old Italian friend, saying that no-one had ever mentioned the Calabrian's name in his presence. It would not be easy to find him, but Federico enjoyed a challenge.

Then Vincent returned to Washington and reclaimed his real identity. Just to be on the safe side, he would play no part in the grand finale.

The D.E.A. came to an agreement with the Peruvian government. Coordinated action was planned, all of which took time. The plantation was attacked at dawn by one of the Peruvian army's special anti-guerrilla units, with support from two fighter jets and an armoured battalion. The coca plants were destroyed. Unfortunately, that season's harvest had already been processed and sent to Italy to be refined and sold.

The Shining Path guerrillas were all killed. Comandante Gualtiero was the last to fall. In his pockets, they found a copy of Mao's *Little Red Book* and 20 grams of the purest cocaine.

2

Minuet

10 Corso Como. At the heart of Milan's high life.

Pounding house music. Cocktails and finger food. Gallerists, writers, actresses, big shots. A perfumed den of deceit.

The Engineer was seventy, and kept himself fit with maniacal dedication. He was known as "the Engineer" despite only having qualified as a surveyor, but when you're the man responsible for construction across the western suburbs of Milan, when you provide a living for two thousand families, when you're someone who never has to deal with doors closed in your face or councillors busy in meetings, you don't need to have a stupid degree certificate on the wall for your name to be on everyone's lips, for your face to be on all the front pages and your charisma in everyone's hearts.

And you can be sure that no-one will come out of the

woodwork to remind you of the technical-commercial school
in Corsico where you dropped out in your third year, of your
correspondence-course diploma. Or of the other shady epi-
sodes in your career.

Holding the Engineer's hand was an insipid blonde busily
introducing him left, right and centre. The girl was his daughter Caterina, who was trying to break into the fashion jungle.
She was a good girl but sorely lacking natural talent. So, like a
good father, caring and indulgent, the Engineer allowed himself to be put on display, to let everyone know that there was
real power behind her.

The things you do for your children!

But the Engineer was in a hurry. Sveva had already sent
him three X-rated texts. She had been waiting at the two-
room flat in Brera for half an hour. Sveva was hot. Sveva was
willing.

"I've got an appointment, Cate!"

"Just a little longer, Papà, please!"

Surrounded by a cluster of beautiful people and dressed, as
always, in black, the legendary Italian fashion guru and one-
time left-wing extremist Sandro P. was pontificating.

"My father said, 'Sandro, you and your crazy Maoist friends
will end up handing over the Duomo to the Cossacks!' And
you know what, my friends? He was right. For years, Giorgio
and I, Miuccia and all the rest have been working almost
exclusively for the *mujiks* and their luxury bimbos. They're the

ones keeping us on our feet. So if they want the Duomo, they're welcome to it. They just need to keep paying . . . in hard currency!"

Everyone laughed. Everyone apart from a very tall, very elegant young man, who let slip a remark in a neutral tone of voice.

"They say a lot of that money comes from the Mafia."

Sandro P. shrugged as if to say, None of my business. The others ignored him. And were amazed to see the Engineer, who was known for his composure, turn on the troublemaker.

"What's your point? I'm sorry, but what's a businessman supposed to do? Check where the money comes from? You know very well we all need that money! What should Sandro do? Ask the oligarch who's proudly draping his luxury bimbo in Italian fashion, 'Excuse me, but you didn't get that rich by screwing someone over, did you? Have you been selling arms to the Arabs? A few bars of uranium to some bloodthirsty dictator?' Of course not! It's not his job. Not his, and not mine. The Russian pays, I go to the bank, taxes are deducted, and the profit is guaranteed. It's all within the law."

"If you say so . . ."

The Engineer could see the lad wasn't going to let it go. He had to be one of those bloody annoying idealists who mistakenly believed they'd taken over Milan with their ex-terrorist poseur of a mayor. With the aid of the financial crisis and the second-hand puritanism that had taken hold of the great unwashed. Frustrated people shooting their mouths off. People who don't know what hard work is. But this is just an interlude, my fine young friend. How long can a community carry on with whingers like that in charge? Not long. And so things would go back to working again like before.

"That's right, my friend, within the law! Rather than busting the balls of fine, upstanding people who create wealth and spread it around, the authorities should go after the real enemies . . ."

"Who are?"

"What about the Chinese? Do you realise how many Chinese shops are springing up like mushrooms? And no-one knows where the money comes from. Then there are the illegal traders. Did you know that in the street where I live they're selling fake Louis Vuitton bags for 50 euros? I mean, 50 euros! These are the things that matter. And people aren't stupid, you know. They've got eyes! Sooner or later . . ."

It was like opening a breach in a dam. Sandro P. began to complain about the Finance Police and their suffocating checks. Someone else had a bone to pick with the unions. A woman launched into a eulogy about Milan in days gone by, a city that had disappeared and might never be seen again.

"Oh, but it will, it will!" the Engineer said.

The young man took a glass, muttered a few platitudes and beat a retreat.

Sandro P. made an appointment with Caterina for two

days' time, saying he would be happy to take a look at her latest creations.

"You were great, Papà! Really great! You don't know how much this means to me! I love you, Papà!"

"But who was that shithead? The tall guy?"

"Search me! It's the first time I've seen him. I'll ask around, if you like."

"Well, he can go fuck himself! But now, sorry Cate, I've really got to go."

His duty was done. He was free.

He saw the tall young guy hurrying towards the exit. For a second, he thought of following him. But why? To demand verbal satisfaction, or worse? And to what end? Did he want to moralise or punch his lights out? No point wasting energy. The Engineer had another outlet for that.

The young man's name was Federico Anselmi, and he was a *capitano* in the Finance Police. He was also the old Italian friend of Vincent Hueso, a.k.a. El Norte.

Since Vincent's message had arrived almost three months earlier, the Calabrian had become his obsession. He had looked at hundreds of files. Cross-referenced all kinds of data. Questioned dozens of informers. He had checked airline passenger lists, going over every flight between Italy and anywhere in Central and South America with a fine-toothed comb, and extracted a short list of names. Three of his brightest officers were sifting through them. But nothing, nothing, nothing. So he had hung up his uniform and taken his search out into Milan. Passing himself off as a financial adviser came easily, as finance had been his career choice before he had joined the force. But still nothing, nothing, nothing.

His bosses were grumbling. What about the Chinese? And what about the standard income figures? Compare the income tax filings against those and you could nail some of the usual suspects, for instance the left-wing architect trying it on with a nice little 2,000-euro tax evasion. What about them? But he carried on, ignoring the ostracism and threats of a transfer, disregarding the arrest statistics, failing to respond to summonses to meetings and telling his friends what they could do with their sensible advice.

Some of his bosses were like the Engineer. Victims of the metaphysics of money. At a certain point, money loses any connection to its origins. It becomes immaterial. The ultimate "good", to put it in economic terms.

And how can you argue with "good"?

In fact, money is tangible. Entirely tangible. It has an origin; it develops, follows a specific path and arrives at its destination. Just like cocaine. Capitano Anselmi wanted to turn money back into something concrete.

There is clean money, and there is dirty money. Metaphysics is the great polluter. Metaphysics removes borders, cancels out differences, destroys opposition.

Dirty money is a poisonous snake. You neutralise a snake by

cutting off the flow of venom. There is only one way to do that: you have to crush the head.

The man that Vincent Hueso had told Federico about was the snake's head. He was going to flush him out and crush him.

Sveva claimed to be twenty-three and Lithuanian. She said she had modelled for the top fashion houses. The Engineer had done some checks. Sveva had been born and raised in Parabagio, on the north-western outskirts of Milan. As for photographs, not a single one had turned up. On the other hand, he had come across some fairly explicit videos on YouPorn.

But that was irrelevant. Waiting for him in her little boudoir were kisses, caresses and much more besides – Sveva could perform contortionist's routines to perfection – as well as some exceptionally high-grade cocaine.

"Come on, baby, let's do another line!"

The Engineer was a generous, affectionate client, the best there was. The only problem was that he sometimes overdid it with the blow. That was why Sveva had the good sense to make sure it was never cut with amphetamines but sometimes mixed a few sleeping pills into the powder.

The coke seemed to send out flashes around the room, which was kept in semi-darkness by the soft, reddish light of the lamp.

★

They did their lines together. Sveva took off her white robe and started to work on his thighs.

Coke has its own sort of arcane beauty, the Engineer thought to himself. He liked to think of these evenings with his favourite companion as the culmination of a career built upon good decisions. The sorts of decisions that bring success to those who deserve it.

Success without guilt: what a sublime feeling!

Sveva was a whore, but a whore with a heart of gold.

The ground rules were clear to them both. The Engineer had laid them down at their first meeting. When she had started to come out with the old story of the poor girl who'd emigrated to find an honest job, but instead . . . the Engineer had stopped her immediately: No sob stories, sweetheart! I come here to have a good time. You can leave your grief at home; I've got more than enough of my own.

Sveva was a whore, and there was nothing wrong with that. That was another thing money could buy. And if someone has money, it's not a crime to use it.

They were wrapped in each other's arms when the police broke down the door.

"Well, well, look what a nice little fish we've caught in our net! Hey, Capú, you know who this gentleman is, don't you?"

"Who doesn't? Dammit, though! He's even uglier up close than he looks on T.V.!"

Sveva could not have known it, but Commissario Casetta's men had been on to her for weeks, all because the Public Prosecutor's office had authorised phone taps to investigate a minor politician involved in the inevitable bribery saga. There had been a one-off encounter between Sveva and the politician; she had been the one to stop it going any further. The politician was one of those tight-fisted types and, even worse, lacking in the personal-hygiene department. To his credit, he wasn't interested in coke. But that one hook-up had been enough to put Sveva in the sights of the police. Piecing together her activities on two fronts, sex and drugs, had been child's play for Ispettore Ciani and Sovrintendente Caputo.

So, while the higher echelons discreetly carried on investigating the politician, already imagining the arrest, the press conference and the front-page headlines, or at least top billing in the *Corriere*'s local news section, Ciani and Caputo had decided to conduct a raid "pursuant to article 41 of the Law on Public Safety, based on the suspicion that the aforementioned Verbena Chiara, a.k.a. Sveva, was holding weapons and/or drugs in her dwelling situated in Via di Brera, 37". No-one had thought that there would be any weapons. But they did find drugs. The presence of a big noise like the Engineer was the icing on the cake.

But was it icing on the cake or a pain in the arse?

The Engineer politely requested permission to get dressed.

"Stay where you are and don't move."

The Engineer stopped what he was doing, smiling vaguely.

Looks like he was a tough one, then! As for Sveva, she showed absolutely no interest in hiding her nakedness. A proper whore, that one. Did she think it would excite them? In any case, she was showing that she could hold it together. To tell the truth, she was also a nice piece of . . .

"We're not doing anything wrong, *commissario*."

"*Ispettore*."

"Pardon me, *Ispettore*. We were just having an enjoyable evening."

Ciani pointed to the coke.

"What about that?"

"Personal use."

Ciani and Caputo burst out laughing. Personal use! Even out there in the open, laid out in neat lines on the little bedside table, there had to be at least 5 or 6 grams. Perhaps if they searched a bit harder, they'd find the same amount again. In any case, supplying even a pinch of the stuff, even gratis, came under the offence "set out and punished by article 73 of Presidential Decree 309/90". Anyway, the current circumstances would be hard to describe as "gratis", given the situation and people involved.

The Engineer cleared his throat.

"Perhaps we might come to some agreement?"

The policemen looked at each other.

Ciani thought of the twenty years he had spent on the streets, rooting around in the city's dirt. Twenty years of human misery, insults and frustration. He thought about his minimal career prospects and the government's recent cost-cutting. About the 2,700 euros he brought home each month, which would soon be whittled down even further, what with the impending cuts to overtime. He thought about their three-room apartment in Quarto Oggiaro, for which they were saddled with a 100,000-euro mortgage at a fixed rate of 4.5 per cent. About his three children, two of them at the commer-cial-technical school, the third with dreams of becoming a ballerina, enrolled in a private ballet school that cost an arm and a leg.

Caputo, meanwhile, was thirty and had been a policeman for seven years. He lived with his girlfriend, a researcher in modern literature on a short-term contract, in two rooms in Sesto San Giovanni. The rent swallowed half his salary, and getting a mort-gage was a pipe dream, since no bank anywhere would lend to a couple in their disastrous situation. The idea of having children had been put on hold even before it had come up.

And why were things this way?

Because some people have too much and some have too little. Some have everything, some nothing.

O.K. But now they had the opportunity to right a few wrongs.

So why weren't they doing what needed to be done?

The two policemen kept on looking at each other, their thoughts converging.

They imagined the consequences of the raid as if it were one of those T.V. series they watched in the evenings, having come home totally shattered. The arrest. The outcry. The trial. The Engineer swearing on his children's lives: "It was a moment of weakness." The Engineer's lawyers ripping them to shreds on the witness stand. Sveva taking responsibility for everything. The Engineer calling a press conference after his acquittal to protest against police violence.

Not much of a story. Above all, the moral message was dubious. What kind of example would it set? A negative one, for sure: that money allows the rich to do whatever they like. Even buy themselves impunity. And the poor keep on getting screwed.

That wasn't the way to right wrongs.

The two policemen stopped looking at each other, and, with a nod, they went to work.

Ciani ordered the Engineer to snort a fat line of coke and then simulate sex with Sveva. Caputo filmed the scene on his phone. The Engineer was permitted to get dressed. Ciani collected all the coke and money, including the cash Sveva had just received from the Engineer. When the girl started to protest, a slap from Caputo sent her sprawling across the bed. They agreed with the Engineer that they would return the video in exchange for a single payment of 100,000 euros. In cash.

Finally, they said their goodbyes and returned to the station.

Their report stated, "Search outcome: Negative."

The Engineer honoured his debt, handing over a small suitcase filled with 500-euro notes to Ciani during the interval of a conference on "Free-market strategies for employment".

Ciani and Caputo returned the video, although with the future looking uncertain and the recession closing in, they kept a copy.

As for the cocaine they had seized, 15 grams in all, they shared it out like good brothers should.

After all, the white shit had its uses.

Sveva and her boyfriend Carlo bought their stuff from the Brambati brothers in Lorenteggio. They usually bought 300 or 400 grams on credit, paying for it with 75 per cent of the proceeds when they sold it on. Not big business but reliable. Sveva and Carlo regularly creamed off around 5 per cent of their takings. A little at a time, so the Brambatis would not get suspicious. The excess was poured into the bottomless pit of debt that Carlo had fallen into with a loan shark in Bovisa, vainly attempting to keep afloat the little tattoo parlour he had opened in Corso Buenos Aires a few years before.

But the misadventure with the police scuppered them. They already owed the Brambati brothers 15,000 euros and had no idea how to get back on track.

They explained the situation to the brothers, who laughed in their faces. It was not their problem. The brothers had kept their side of the bargain and delivered the stuff. Now they expected payment.

"Just give me a bit more," Carlo begged. "We'll sell it on as usual and you can keep everything. We've always been good workers, you know that."

"Always? The word means nothing to me, dickhead," Luca Brambati said. Luca was the more aggressive and unpredictable of the two brothers. "You've got a week to sort it out, otherwise you're in the shit."

"How am I going to find 15,000 euros in a week?"

"You could sell that hole where you put holes in other people," Pippo Brambati laughed. He acted the wise, understanding brother but was actually the bigger bastard of the two.

"Like I haven't thought about it! It's all mortgaged!"

"That's not our problem. Tell Sveva to get out and suck some more cock – that slut's got real talent!" Luca cut him off.

"You could do a bank," Pippo suggested.

"Or you could sell the bitch to the Albanians," Luca said.

The week went by. Carlo worked like a madman at the tattoo parlour. Sveva started hooking at 9.00 in the morning, knocked off at 9.00 at night and then moved on to stag dos. She even managed to fit in an orgy for a bunch of rich Russians. Their combined total came to 10,000 euros. Carlo handed over the loot to the Brambati brothers at their bar in Lorenteggio.

"There's five thousand missing," Luca said, after counting the notes.

"That's all I've got!"

"But it's not everything you owe us," Pippo said, puzzled.

"Give me a few more days. Where's the harm? You've seen I'll be good for it. Just a few days!"

"We'll let you know," the brothers told him.

Carlo returned home to reassure Sveva. There was no need to be frightened. The Brambatis had everything to gain from waiting a while. With a bit of luck, they'd pull through this time as well.

But two days later, with the streets full of shoppers, Carlo and Sveva were shot dead. A bullet to the back of the head. By two hitmen on motorbikes, in full-face helmets and black leathers. They rode off unhindered through the incoherent shouting of the crowd.

3

Jig

Don Achille Patriarca smoked his cigar and waited.

Mico and Rocco would be arriving in a few minutes.

In the meantime, he smoked and he thought.

Don Achille was president of Buccinasco's "Antonino Scopelliti" social club, a refuge for housewives, pensioners and a few hard-up families in need of help and comfort.

The club was a recognised source of civic pride and a flagship for the local authorities, whatever their politics.

It was the perfect place to meet and talk business freely: after all, it was named after a heroic magistrate killed by the Mafia.

Now that was a genuine, authentic touch of class.

It was very hot in the courtyard, but Don Achille wouldn't have gone without his cigar for all the gold in the world.

Obviously, smoking was prohibited inside. As the club's ultimate authority, he was extremely strict when it came to
abiding by and enforcing the law.

A toothless old man named Brusagatti came over to say
hello. A former accountant, he still insisted on using the appropriate title, *ragioniere*.

Don Achille responded with a warm, friendly smile.

"Have you heard the latest? Those murders . . . what's hap-
pening to this city, I ask you?!"

"They're no better than animals, those murderers, animals."

"Don't you think we ought to have the death penalty?"

"Undoubtedly! But not before they've been tortured!"

"You couldn't spare a cigar, could you? Just now I . . ."

"*Ragioniere*, you know you mustn't smoke! With your
heart . . ."

"How many more fucking years . . . Pardon my language!
How much longer do you reckon I'm going to live? And you
can't spare me a cigar?"

"But what if your wife found out? How would I look
then?"

"Oh come on, I know how to keep my mouth shut."

In the end, the old man got his Toscanello, but seemed to
have no plans to make himself scarce. Don Achille realised that
the man had something to ask him and was trying to pluck up
the courage. The little farce was threatening to drag on and on.
Better to grab the bull by the horns.

"What's the problem, *ragioniere*?"

"It's my grandson. You know Luigi?"

"The tall, brown-haired boy who sometimes comes to collect you in his car?"

"That's him. Well, he's started to go off the rails. I thought that you, with your authority and eloquence, might be able to . . ."

"Consider it done, *ragioniere*!"

Brusagatti finally took his leave, but not before thanking Don Achille profusely.

Don Achille relit his cigar.. How he loved the taste of the cold ash coming back to life!

As a man of honour, Don Achille saw Milan as conquered territory and the Milanese as weak-minded fools. Good at making the money go round, hard workers, certainly, but profoundly ignorant of the ways of the world. But perhaps he was wrong. Brusagatti, for example, had approached him with the same deference as any minion back home. As if he knew. And perhaps he did. Perhaps he knew and accepted it because it suited him to do so.

Perhaps the whole of Milan knew. And the whole of Milan accepted it. Because it suited them to do so.

Don Achille was a small, dark, compact man. He always wore a jacket and tie, and an old black beret as a reminder of his time in the mountains. His lucky charm.

The *don* spoke little, but his word was law in Corsico, Buccinasco and the Milanese hinterland.

The Brambati brothers had become a pain in the arse. With this latest stunt, they had gone too far.

After the murder of those two wretches, the tattoo artist and his whore, Milan had woken up feeling dirty and corrupt. It had been a rude awakening.

People found out that the two victims were being investigated for drug dealing.

So now everyone was up in arms about cocaine.

The politicians had got themselves worked up. The right laid the blame on left-wing culture and its notoriously permissive ways. The left replied that cocaine, the drug of efficiency and speed, was nothing to do with them.

These little spats left Don Achille indifferent. He had never set foot in a polling station. But for years he had been paying off and manipulating politicians on all sides, giving his people orders to vote this way or that, according to convenience. He wasn't interested in politics, and truth be told, politics disgusted him.

The point was elsewhere. It was about business. The only thing that counted in this world. For business to run smoothly, you need peace. Especially in a place like Milan. From the outside, it looks like a beautiful woman wearing refined clothes, all *haute couture* and seductive glances, but underneath, the city has the soul of a passive housewife. Milan wants action, but most of all it wants to let things happen. Looking the other way, if necessary. In a spirit of reciprocal and shared convenience.

Hypocrites. They're swimming in cocaine.

And yet. And yet. If those dickheads start shooting in the city centre at rush hour, leaving two people dead on the pavement . . . and if one of the victims is a woman, which gets public opinion going . . . then Milan can no longer pretend not to see. So the authorities had been quick to proclaim a "crackdown". There had been a meeting of the Committee for Public Order and Security. There had been talk of sending in a special investigations unit. A hell of a fuss.

Don Achille knew that these were problems which would pass. Before long, the double murder would be forgotten like any others, and life would go back to normal.

Unless those dickheads pulled another stunt. Don Achille knew all about the rush of blood to the head that the boys got after doing a job. The rush of invincibility, the adrenalin coursing through your veins that demands more action. Don Achille had come up from the street. He too had been young once. But luckily for him, he'd had great teachers: he'd been raised by the elders of the *'ndrina*, who encouraged him when he needed pushing, held him back when he went too far and punished him when he did wrong.

Wise and inflexible teachers, strict but understanding.

If only those impulsive kids had talked to him first.

Take Mico and Rocco. They were good boys. Boys who knew the ways of the world, who would do well for themselves one day. But only because they had been lucky enough to be born in the right place, the right family. When Mico, for instance, had been about to go off the rails, Don Achille had needed to intervene.

The others had not been so lucky. And because they did not recognise authority, they were heading for a fall.

And so . . . Perhaps, perhaps, Don Achille thought, we must also accept a share of the responsibility. He had opposed the idea of "opening up" the cocaine business along free-market lines. Finding himself in the minority, he had bowed his head, as his people had learned to do thousands of years ago. Now the 'ndrine bought the harvest directly from the Mexican cartels, the leaves still on the plants, and took on the risks associated with transporting it. The consignments were refined along the way, during stop-offs in friendly countries or right there in the hinterland. The stuff was sold in bulk to intermediaries with connections to trusted families who then subdivided it further, portioned it off and so on. Dealing was completely out of their hands now. Don Achille had to admit that the profits had snow-balled, but a measure of anarchy had also been introduced.

The market was too huge to be controlled.

And the two who had died, Carlo and Sveva, were no-bodies.

What had they died for? Five thousand euros!

Above them were the Brambatis, themselves small fry.

Small, but with sharp teeth and too much ambition.

The Brambatis were going around telling people that justice had been done.

Don Achille found this intolerable.

What the Brambatis had done was not justice. It was madness. For a 5,000-euro mistake, you sent a warning, you set fire to a car, or, at the most, the very most, you broke an arm.

But they had killed people.

The Brambati brothers had to be done away with.

Given everything that was at stake with the Mexicans, the mess had to be nipped in the bud.

"Here you are at last, my boys!"

Smiling broadly, Don Achille walked over to Mico and Rocco.

Mico drove carefully along the unpaved road, avoiding the potholes but finding it difficult to see due to the unseasonable fog rising from the banks of the Olona River. Luca Brambati, sitting next to him, was singing "La Bamba" at the top of his voice between lines of coke. Luca never went anywhere without his fringed leather bag. It had been given to him on his first trip to South America by a Puerto Rican dealer called Rudy Peña. Luca carried his stash in it, plus a few thousand euros that he liked to flash to impress the local kids.

In the back seat, reminiscing about their joint escapades

back in the day, Pippo kept on saying how great it was to meet up again after so many years, that they were friends for life, that now they were back together it would be for good, that they were going to start where they had left off, get back on track, wasn't that right, Micú my brother? Rocco remained quiet, coiling the thin rope hidden beneath the blanket over his knees "because I'm still not used to this fucking fog".

Mico braked suddenly a few metres from a derelict farmhouse. Their destination, where they had stashed the getaway motorbike.

"I think I've taken a wrong turn," he said quietly, glancing at the rear-view mirror.

That was their signal.

Rocco threw off the blanket, grabbed the rope and twisted it around Luca's neck. Luca cried out, tried to get his fingers round the rope, reared up and shattered the window deflector with an elbow. The little bag slipped from his grasp, flew out of his hand.

Mico stuck the knife in his side, and Luca's body went limp. Rocco carried on tightening as the resistance ebbed away.

Pippo was still paralysed by shock and fear when Mico turned round and aimed the .32 automatic at the centre of his forehead.

He pulled back the slide. Pippo's eyes filled with tears.

"Mico . . . brother . . ."

That's right, brother. Brother Judas.

They had met in their second year at Giuseppe Garibaldi

Middle School, immediately recognising each other as kindred spirits. Mico, Rocco and Pippo had become inseparable. They started off by spreading shit on their desks during their hated maths lesson, then cemented their friendship by systematically extorting the younger kids' sweets. A couple of years later, Luca had joined the gang. Almost immediately, they had all stopped turning up at school, moving on to minor theft, brawling and threatening people with knives. One time, they stole a Porsche and went whoring in Bovisa. A couple of bigger jobs, at a jeweller's and a *bureau de change*, had brought in the cash that allowed them to buy themselves a Porsche and swap the hookers for stunning eastern European escort girls. They were living the good life. Best of all was the friendship: sharing risks, covering each other's backs, that wonderful, heart-warming sense of protection, when you know there's someone who will never betray you and who feels the same about you.

Rocco let go of Luca's inert body.

"I'm done with this one, Mico. What the fuck are you waiting for?"

"Shut up!"

"Fuck's sake, someone might see us!"

"I told you to shut up!"

"If you don't do it I will, partner," Rocco said, sticking his neck out.

Mico looked askance at him. Rocco put up his hands. Fair

enough. Mico was the older of the two, and Rocco had to obey him. O.K. But Don Achille had given them both the job. If they failed, they would both have failed.

"I'll give you three minutes, then I'll do it myself."

Pippo had put his hands together, as if in prayer.

"Let me go, Mico. I've got some money put aside. I'll go to Brazil. I'll make myself scarce. Fuck, I messed up. I mean fuck, I shouldn't have killed those two, fuck! But you understand, Mico. There was coke involved, a lot of coke, and I couldn't just let it go. Come on, Mico, my brother . . ."

At a certain point, Pippo had started to get heavily into coke. Then they had got caught at a roadblock. In the glove box were 5 or 6 grams. Pippo took the rap. Neither Luca nor Mico paid a fine. But the news got back to Don Achille.

The good times were over.

The *don* called Mico to Corsico, fed him a lunch of baby goat and Cirò red, and then reminded him, because evidently the boy had forgotten, who he was, where he came from, how much he owed the family and what the family expected of him.

"A real man *sells* coke, or *bamba*, as the Milanese dickheads call it. If need be, but only if absolutely necessary, he might taste it, but he doesn't *use* it. Ever. Because coke turns you into a slave, and a real man is born to be a master, not a servant. So, Micuzzu, keep your head on your shoulders, and no more fucking about."

Mico listened, made himself small and humble, held back the sobs he could feel rising in his throat, made no attempt to justify himself, kissed the *don*'s hand, and that very evening, after a memorable dinner of oysters and champagne, he said goodbye to the Brambati brothers for ever.

All that had happened five years ago. Back then, he had felt like a god.

Now they were ordering him to play Judas.

The three minutes had passed. The situation was threatening to become embarrassing. Interrupting his partner's reverie, Rocco took out his .38 and prepared to shoot Pippo.

Mico awoke from his trance. It was down to him.

"Bye, Pippo," he murmured, then squeezed the trigger.

Rocco nodded, reassured, and put down his weapon.

Without saying a word, they got out of the car, opened the boot, and took out the helmets, canisters and petrol bombs. Mico stripped the .32; Rocco doused the bodies and the car with petrol, lit the Molotov cocktails and threw them in. They waited for the fire to take hold, ran to the bike, put on their helmets and sped off towards Milan, only stopping to consign the guns, the rope and the knife to the river's welcoming waters.

Rocco and Mico thought of themselves as professionals.

But even the most seasoned professionals suffered from the occasional oversight.

Rocco had not noticed that Luca Brambati's little bag had fallen out of the car.

Mico had unwittingly kicked it away, meaning that it escaped the fire.

It was found by two kids who raced out of the ruined house while the roar of the bike's engine could still be heard.

The boy and girl, very young and still living with their parents, came to the house to make love because they were too poor to rent a room by the hour or hide anywhere else. Their expressions alternated between terror, relief and uncertainty. Just before reaching the farmhouse they had almost quarrelled. He had wanted to park their little Reiju scooter, which had cost her four months shut up in a dreadful call centre, about a hundred metres away.

"Someone might see us."

"Who? No-one ever comes out here . . ."

"A passing car. The driver sees the scooter by the farmhouse, gets ideas in his head and . . ."

"Don't be such a chicken."

"I'm only being careful."

"I'll get my boots dirty!"

"Then we'll clean them off!"

She had decided there was something profoundly unfair about the world if two young lovers were forced to hide like rats just because they were guilty of being poor. The thought reduced her to tears of rage and disappointment, and he gently consoled her. It would not last for ever. He was an apprentice mechanic, and everyone said he had a way with engines. One day, he would have a workshop of his own, and then . . .

In the end, she let herself be persuaded. They were in love, dammit, and their desire to be together was too strong!

Now she was thanking him: it was down to his caution that they were still alive.

But what should they do? The car was burning, and from their hiding place they had seen the pistol and heard the shot. It did not take a lot of imagination to work out what had happened.

Their first impulse was to leave. Run to the scooter and forget everything they had witnessed.

"We could call the police," she suggested.

"Are you mad? Once they start with their questions, it never ends. Why were you here? And how come it happened like that and not like this . . . ? And listen, it's none of our business!"

Then he noticed the little bag. Peeking inside, they saw the money and the coke.

"Oh my God, get rid of it and let's get out of here!" she said, terrified.

"Hold on, let me see . . . there must be at least 5,000 euros here!"

"It's cursed, that money. Let's go!"

It was the right thing to do, and he knew it.

But dammit, with 5,000 euros he would have a deposit. Then he could have a workshop all of his own! No more bosses, no more struggling. A workshop of his own! And that white powder . . . he knew a couple of local lads who'd give him good money for it. Reliable types who wouldn't go shooting their mouths off. So he'd be able to add the first month's rent to the down payment.

"I'm taking this stuff."

"Are you crazy?"

"No-one's going to come looking for it, don't worry. And I know what to do with it!"

She let herself be convinced once again. It always ended the same way. Because she trusted him, and because her fear had given way in the face of an exciting adventure.

He stashed the little bag under his jacket, and they climbed onto the scooter and took off.

The blaze was spotted by Maresciallo Misilmeri, patrol leader of radio unit 16 in the operations section of the Varese *carabinieri*. And, who knows why, perhaps due to a policeman's intuition or a suspicion of young people caused by years turning sour on the job, it occurred to him that perhaps the two kids he had just passed on their scooter might know something about it. So Misilmeri sounded the alert, and a search bulletin was sent out from operations H.Q.

But the flying squad car that spotted the scooter on the

outskirts of Busto Arsizio belonged to the state police, not the *carabinieri*. Seeing the uniformed men signalling to him to stop, the boy panicked and naively tried to get rid of the bag. In doing so, he lost control of the bike, which skidded off the road. Both he and the girl fell badly. Luckily, they were wearing their helmets, but when they tried to stand up, dazed and shocked, they found themselves in the sights of three gleaming Beretta submachine guns.

The boy put his hands up, burst into tears and told the police the truth.

Naturally, he was not believed. In the meantime, Maresciallo Misilmeri had announced over the radio that two bodies had been found in the burning car. It was natural for the policemen to think that the young lovers were responsible. The fact that they were clean-cut kids with no criminal record proved nothing. When you work on the streets, you soon learn not to trust appearances.

The truth started to acquire a certain weight when the first reports from forensics landed on the Public Prosecutor's desk. Although the bodies were partially burned, enough had been salvaged to be able to attribute the double murder to professionals. And the two kids on the scooter were anything but that. The prints taken from a miraculously intact thumb put a name to the corpse that, as the final report stated, "had belonged in life to one Luca Brambati, a criminal previously charged with offences against property, murder, attempted murder and drug trafficking". In the circumstances, the other dead man could only be his brother Pippo, not least because the two notorious cut-throats from Lorenteggio had disappeared on the same evening as the murder. Finally, ballistic tests proved that the two kids had not fired any weapons.

The deputy prosecutor leading the investigation questioned the boy one last time. More than anything out of thoroughness, because releasing him was the only option.

That was how a crucial detail emerged at the end of yet another interrogation report.

"Now that I think about it, Your Honour, I recognised the bike the two men were riding. It was a Harley Davidson Iron 883. A customised bike, painted green; you don't see many like it."

The boy was right.

It really was an unusual bike. There were only seven in the whole of Lombardy. One belonged to a man with no criminal record. A plumber in Buccinasco by the name of Santo Perrino.

He was the nephew of Don Achille Patriarca.

4

Sarabande

Don Achille Patriarca was an extremely cautious man. He owned neither a mobile phone nor a personal computer. In his substantial house there were just two old landline phones, which he only used for mundane tasks. "Sensitive" communication was conducted in person, or via the tried and trusted system of passing notes invented by his Sicilian cousins. It might have been his old gangster's sixth sense, or the paranoia that goes hand in hand with the life of a mafioso, but since all the fuss had started, Don Achille had felt the dogs snapping at his heels.

So he had stepped up his precautions.

He had ordered a suspension of contacts between clan members until further notice, unless they were absolutely necessary. The last-ditch solution was the little church of San Terenzio, which was run with a firm hand by Padre Piscopo.

The fiery young parish priest had a traditionalist bent and was extremely good at inflaming his congregations with thundering sermons denouncing moral degeneration. Housewives and pensioners went home with tears in their eyes, shaken to their very cores by vivid images of the eternal punishment that, the priest assured them, would be visited on women who aborted their babies or on fornicating homosexuals.

Padre Piscopo was a reliable messenger for the clan and the person to whom Don Achille turned when it became necessary to contact Tano. The *don* wanted the young banker to reassure him regarding the fate of the money invested in the business with the Mexicans. He had been shaken by newspaper and T.V. reports of the armed attack on Peru's largest cocaine plantation. The money they had invested belonged to the *mamma*, and Don Achille was responsible for it in the eyes of God and Man.

Padre Piscopo received the message and passed it on.

Tano Raschillà and Don Achille met at midday Mass on the first Sunday of September. Tano told the *don* what he wanted to hear: that the money was safe, that the business with El Rubio was continuing on another plantation, and that profitable solutions were being investigated for the capital, which was being held temporarily at the bank in the Turks and Caicos.

The *don* was pleased. He dispensed a few pieces of good advice – get married, but to a good, God-fearing girl; have children, because children are the manna of the Lord; carry on working for the family; and keep on studying alongside the other business – before giving the talented youngster his blessing and bringing the meeting to a close.

Don Achille had chosen the church because a meeting in a holy place is always neutral, and even if they were following him and had managed to identify Tano, there was nothing to suggest that the two men's being together in such a place was in any way suspect.

Don Achille was right to be cautious. Since his family connection to the plumber whose Harley Davidson had "almost certainly" been used in a double homicide had emerged, his personal file, full of notes yet short of convictions, had started circulating again within the Anti-Mafia Investigation Department.

So Don Achille was under surveillance. Followed and bugged around the clock. And anyone in contact with him was also put under the microscope by the department.

As a result, his meeting with Tano was duly registered, and the young man was identified as "Gaetano Raschillà, aged thirty-two, banker". The officer on duty made a quick check and wrote a note stating, "Nothing has emerged in relation to the subject, who appears to be of good moral and civil conduct, is not involved in penal proceedings past or present, and belongs to a family unconnected to organised crime activities." There were now dozens of similar notes in an investigation that seemed to have run aground. The officer had his note approved by his superior, as was the procedure, and passed it on to the other investigative bodies for further checks, which he considered unnecessary.

That was how a name set alarm bells ringing and came to land on the desk of Capitano Federico Anselmi of the Finance Police.

Raschillà. It sounded familiar. But from where, when, why?

It took days of patient research, days of torturing his brain cells, but finally the link emerged.

Gaetano Raschillà. It was there in black and white on the airline manifests. Raschillà had been in South America when El Rubio had had his meeting with a Calabrian. Federico took another couple of days and did more checking. There had been a specific purpose to his journey: to give a speech on the welfare crisis to an international conference in Mexico City.

It seemed the perfect excuse for a meeting between narcos and traffickers.

But of course it could just have been a series of deplorable coincidences.

There was only one way to find out.

Federico got hold of a series of snapshots of Raschillà, scanned them and sent them to Vincent Hueso's confidential email address.

El Norte skyped him back fifteen minutes later.

"It's him, my friend. I don't know how the fuck you did it, but you got him."

"Are you sure?"

"I'm already composing a *cop-corrido* in your honour."

Federico went down to the bar on the corner by the Provincial Headquarters and knocked back three whiskies, one after the other.

Straight after that, he called Terry, the well-endowed journalist he had been seeing for a week, and called off their date for that evening. She was not happy. He came up with the excuse of an emergency shift, but she cut him off coldly: she could happily go to the Subsonica concert on her own, but as for coming back alone, that was another question. An open question.

Federico bought the bottle of whisky, went back to his office, grabbed the papers he needed and closeted himself in his little bachelor's apartment overlooking the Porta Romana.

Terry was right: there was an open question.

But it was not about matters of the heart. It was about a sharp-suited *'ndranghetista* bastard and the best way to bring him down as hard as possible. Federico turned on his computer. In the investigative archives he found nothing. Raschillà was a complete unknown. Then he visited a few financial sites, where the man was described as a young wizard in the world of investment banking.

There was only one thing that would entice a man like Gaetano Raschillà to rub shoulders with narcos, guerrillas and *campesinos* on a Peruvian plantation.

A financial transaction.

But for someone above suspicion and of that calibre to go out there, it had to be something really huge.

But how big?

A while back they had caught someone working for Montreal's Bonavolontà family. He was moving one and a half billion dollars. In terms of Mafia hierarchy, the Bonavolontà were a small-to-medium-scale clan. Nonetheless, they had been able to put together 1.5 billion U.S. dollars.

According to anti-Mafia investigators, the Patriarca clan were at the top of the pile in the cocaine business in Northern Italy. So how much could they make?

Federico roughed out a calculation, taking into account the amount of cocaine that could have been imported, and its market value after it had been refined and cut, minus losses from small-scale seizures.

The figures that emerged made his head spin.

He had to get his hands on that money.

He emptied the bottle and went to bed.

The next day he was in Rome, for a meeting with the *comandante generale*.

Officially on leave, he made his preparations from a safe house in Via Meda provided by the Anti-Mafia Department. He bought two domain names and filled the sites with fabricated information, building an imaginary autobiography from scratch, creating a legend, just as he had done in the past. It had worked before and it would work again. There was no reason for it not to. In any case, all he needed were a few face-to-face meetings with his man.

After a couple of weeks had passed, he requested and was granted an appointment with the financier.

The "Raschillà and Partners" office occupied 320 square metres on the third floor of a little building in the heart of Milan's financial district. It was staffed by lawyers and accountants as well as a number of consultants, interns, secretaries and clerks. Tano Raschillà received his prospective client in his office, Federico having introduced himself as Gianni Bruni.

Forty square metres with a view of the Foro Bonaparte, soundproof glass, air conditioning, a Sottsass lamp, Frau sofas and chairs, and a lithograph from Cascella's French period. There was more: a classic chaise-longue, a small piece by Alighiero e Boetti on a white wall, and a wonderful untitled painting by Mimmo Paladino, a yellow face staring out from a chestnut-brown background. Federico imagined it might represent a Samnite warrior on the eve of his last battle. An image of strength and desperation. But now he would take the role of the Roman legions.

Raschillà clearly had good taste, and no expense had been spared in furnishing his lair. But then he could afford it. He worked for the world's sixth-largest economic power. A power unaffected by economic crises or shrinking turnovers, a power that needn't worry about unions or balance sheets, that ensures a constant turnover of leaders . . . and its profits never stop rising. Organised crime. The epitome of free-market economics.

"You asked to see me, Dottor Bruni."

"Indeed. I represent a group of investors who would prefer to remain anonymous."

"May I ask how you came to choose me?"

"Your name was mentioned by people whose trustworthiness is beyond question."

The message was more than clear. Tano Raschillà remained impassive. Federico placed his white leather briefcase on the desk, clicked open the lock and pushed the whole thing over to Raschillà. The banker glanced at the contents. Still no reaction.

"That's $800,000 in Federal Reserve bearer bonds," "Dottor" Bruni said with an empty smile.

Raschillà examined a couple of the bonds.

"A bit out of date, it would appear."

"But still valid."

"You know better than I do," Raschillà sighed, "that sometimes this type of bond is used in what we might call . . . unorthodox transactions."

Listen to this hypocrite! Federico answered his objection with a shrug.

"Think of this as a small advance, Dottor Raschillà."

"I'll have to make some checks."

"Take all the time you need. I'll leave the bonds with you."

Not waiting for a reply, Federico handed Raschillà his card, turned on his heel and walked out.

Five days went by.

Federico had no doubt that the bonds would pass the test: they were part of a stock of bearer bonds issued by the Federal Reserve in the 1930s and stolen in 1968 by the Weathermen, a group of American terrorists who had wanted to smash the capitalist system, starting in their own backyard. The police had found them by chance two months earlier while searching the house of an ageing villain who had been linked to the Vallanzasca gang. The news of their rediscovery had been kept secret, and they had been passed to Federico under authorisation from the *comandante generale*. There could be problems if the investigator's real identity emerged in the course of Raschillà's checks. Or if that old fox Don Achille decided to block the deal. But on the one hand, the bad guys would need to be outrageously lucky to catch him out, and anyway Federico trusted human greed implicitly.

His trust was repaid. Tano Raschillà made his checks, and the fake trail laid by Federico led him directly to a nest of companies based in Kiev in Ukraine. Bonds that were valid, if a bit dated, combined with Ukrainian capital: it smelled of Mafia. Tano was excited by the idea that he had been contacted by an emissary from the powerful organisations of the East. There was no need to inform Don Achille. The family had done a lot for him. But there had never been any talk of membership. In fact, Don Achille had explained several times, with great lucidity, that the best thing for everyone was for Tano to continue to do his job out in the open, above suspicion, like the good professional he was.

Tano finally made the call, and Federico returned to the office on the Foro Bonaparte, this time welcomed with broad smiles.

Four more meetings followed, and more bearer bonds were handed over. Tano suggested a double investment strategy, looking at short-term, high-yield funds to start with. Obviously, the risk was high, but they would have to trust him. On the other hand, there was the possibility of acquiring stakes in insolvent companies within the consortium working on the high-speed railway line between Turin and Lyon. This was the best way, Tano assured Federico, to guarantee that the capital would be absolutely untraceable.

"I will have to talk to my backers, Dottor Raschillà."

"Of course, Dottor Bruni."

"Good. I leave for Kiev tomorrow morning. I ought to be able to sort things out in five or six days. I'll see you when I get back."

"You are always welcome, *dottore*."

"Would you call me a taxi, please? I've given my driver the evening off."

"I wouldn't dream of it! I'll drive you myself!"

So, thanks to Tano's generosity or, more accurately, his greed, once installed in the Audi Q4, Federico was able to connect a "diagnostic tool" to the O.B.D.-II connector, allowing him to monitor the banker's communications whenever he was on the move.

In the meantime, taking advantage of a young secretary whose indolence was matched by her unfamiliarity with even the most basic principles of caution, he had the latest generation of spyware installed on the firm's P.C.s and mobiles.

Like a good fisherman with his lines set, he waited.

He did not have to wait long.

Three days.

And then he intercepted two apparently innocuous emails.

From: t.ras@trasandpartners.it
To: Wilson@Intertradebank.uk

Re: log in ref.Bounty 676

From: Wilson@Intertradebank.uk
To: t.ras@trasandpartners.it

Re: log in confirmed

If he had not lost his touch, if he was not due for the scrap heap, if he had not got everything wrong, that was an order to transfer a sum of money. He logged into the databases he was entitled to access, as well as those he was able to hack thanks to lessons he'd received years earlier from a Danish hacker with whom he had had his usual brief and tempestuous fling. The Intertrade Bank had its headquarters in London, but its subsidiaries were concentrated on Providenciales in the Turks and Caicos Islands, a tax haven that operated with Her Majesty's blessing.

"Wilson" stood for Wilson Collins, the director of one of the subsidiaries.

The reference number identified the transaction but not the account number.

There was only one legal way to obtain that.

A formal international request through the courts.

But that would not work.

Just as it had not worked three years earlier.

Three years earlier.

Federico and Vincent had, almost simultaneously, closed in on half a million dollars'-worth of dirty money laundered by a fixer in Turin through an account with City Lights Bank in the Cayman Islands.

That was when they had met for the first time. They had hit it off and decided to work together.

Posing as merchant bankers, they built up a sham company, both bringing with them non-existent funds from imaginary subscribers, and opened an account at City Lights Bank. Thanks to Vincent, they were able to wangle goodwill with the local police. Go in, take what you want, and get lost quick. We haven't seen anything.

One fine day, they visited Mr O'Hara, the director, and presented him with a sequestration order.

O'Hara was a sprightly Irishman on the brink of drawing his pension who dreamt of retiring to a farm in Donegal. Retaining his composure, he led the two men to the vault in a town centre basement.

There, a calm-looking computer nerd from Bangalore explained contritely that a sudden inexplicable problem with the operating system had wiped all their hard disks. Searching the director's office a few minutes later, Vincent discovered the alarm: a small, insignificant-looking button on the floor, concealed by a crease in the ugly locally produced rug, to the left of the little couch from which Mr O'Hara ran his lucrative business.

An insignificant detail.

That was the problem with the legal approach: it almost never worked.

Because the bastards didn't give a shit about the rules, and that made them fast, really fast. Too fast.

So he had to find another way.

Grand Finale

Sissy, the prodigiously capable secretary whom Mr Collins trusted more than he trusted himself, came in without knocking. Unprecedented. This had never happened in ten years of their working closely together. To justify such a serious breach of etiquette, it had to be something serious. Sissy was a native of Providenciales, with wide hips and a maternal smile, but the expression on her plump features did not bode well.

"It's the Italian."

"Tell me."

"He's transferred his funds."

"How much?"

"He's emptied the account, left just ten thousand to keep it open. The rest . . . pffft! Up in smoke!"

Collins rubbed his bald pate.

"When?"

"Last night."

Collins sprang to his feet.

"Last night, huh? It can't have been him! Someone's broken into the system! Lock everything down! All transactions are suspended until further notice! Get me the head of security . . . now!"

"I'm afraid there's no point, sir."

"What do you mean, 'no point'?"

"The order came from the account holder. The password was entered correctly. There has been no breach of the system. Mr Raschillà has simply taken back his money."

"I understand. Thank you, Sissy. You may go now."

Sissy shut the door behind her. Running into his small private bathroom, Collins vomited up a mixture of breakfast and bile. He was good at his job. One of the best; everyone said so. His connection with money was somehow . . . mystical. The loss of a two-billion deposit caused him actual physical suffering. He went back to his desk. Where had he gone wrong? He had always treated his very important, decidedly unusual client with the utmost correctness. He had scrupulously respected all instructions. In the whole of the U.K. and its various dependencies, Mr Raschillà could not have found a safer refuge for his capital. Mr Collins had been discreet, able and utterly reserved. He had sent the supervisory authorities scrupulous reports in which he personally guaranteed the propriety of all the transactions on an account that others would have found embarrassing, to say the least. Before exposing himself personally like that, he had secured the necessary authorisations from Head Office. And when Collins had passed on the details of the transaction to London, they had jumped for joy, without stopping to ask too many questions about the origins of their amazing haul.

Now all of this would come back on him.

They were not going to take it well in London.

Back in London, they were happy to keep both eyes shut when it came to money.

But the same eyes would immediately spring open when the money disappeared.

He might as well pack his bags. Next stop: ruination.

He went back to wondering where he had gone wrong. Telling himself over and over again that he had not.

A ray of hope began to emerge. It might have been a temporary transfer. Or a matter of necessity. Perhaps Raschillà had needed to demonstrate his liquidity, so he had taken the money out with the intention of putting it back.

There was only one way to find out.

Signing in to Skype, Collins called Raschillà. It was 8.45 a.m. on Thursday, 27 September.

The time difference between Italy and the Turks and Caicos Islands is seven hours.

It was 3.45 p.m. when Tano Raschillà received Mr Collins' call.

After a few moments, his face went white. He had the message repeated and said he would call back shortly.

Putting on his best phoney smile, he cleared his throat and asked the man sitting opposite to bear with him.

"There's been an emergency. If you will excuse me . . ."

"There's no need to check, Tano. It's all true."

"But . . . what do you mean, it's all true?"

"It was me. I emptied your account."

The man calling himself Dottor Bruni delicately placed his Finance Police I.D. card on the desk.

The young investment-banking wizard looked at the card, with its photograph showing a policeman wearing a wispy beard and the severe expression befitting a servant of the state. He loosened his tie and gasped.

"I don't feel so good."

"Whereas I have never felt better, believe me."

Putting his feet up on the desk and stretching his legs, Federico enjoyed his magic moment.

Three years earlier at the Marriott Hotel on Grand Cayman, he and Vincent had spent an evening getting drunk on rum. As in an old Western movie, it had been an evening of great existential revelations. Vincent had joined the D.E.A. as a proud new American citizen, wanting to free his adopted homeland from the cancer of drugs, because it was down to him to redeem his people. It had not taken him long to find out how things really stood.

"There are two kinds of agent, my friend. The good ones – that's me and five or six other guys – and the pieces of shit – that's everyone else. Who do you think gave the Mexicans carte blanche to flood the streets of our cities with crack and angel dust? The Agency. We did. When we fucked the Colombians we opened a freeway for those bastards. The political big shots call it 'divide and rule'; you ought to know something about that. The truth is that drugs make the world go round, money makes the world go round, and the system keeps running on compromise. Shit, buddy, one day or another, someone's gonna put a bullet in my brain, and you know who it'll be? My room-mate. Or some colleague I'm fucking. This is a stupid war, because it's a phoney war."

"So why are you fighting, then?"

"I don't know anymore. No, wait. I do know. Because I don't want to give in."

Federico put Vincent's outburst down to bitterness over the massive blow they had just suffered. Back then he still believed. Believed in legality, in the state, in a healthy economy. He believed in clean money, which had to be protected from dirty money. That was why he was fighting the drug traffickers. And going after what they valued above all else: their money.

Vincent gave him the kind of look you would reserve for a madman.

The American ended the evening in the arms of two hookers. When Federico went to find him at dawn, his friend discovered that the girls had stolen his wallet.

"You see? It's like I said. You can't trust anyone!"

Over time, Federico had come round to Vincent's point of view.

Trust had been replaced by disillusionment.

The war had become a private battle.

The only reason to carry on fighting was an aesthetic one. The narcos, their shadowy bankers, the go-getting business-men who got high at the weekend, Don Achille and his goons, the street dealers, the whacked-out kids, their brains scrambled by crack, the sluts who would fuck a horse for another fix, this career-criminal fuckhead who was about to take a well-deserved fall . . . they all belonged to the same race. An ugly race that revelled in its own ugliness. For that reason, and for that reason alone, they all needed to be cut down.

It was a matter of aesthetics.

Someone knocked on the door. A young intern appeared, brandishing a file. Raschillà dismissed him with a growl.

"Maybe we could come to an agreement . . ." he said finally.

"That's why I'm here, my friend."

"I could go up to . . . let's say five hundred thousand . . ."

Federico laughed out loud.

"Six hundred," Raschillà said.

"You don't understand," Federico said, cutting him off, suddenly deadly serious. "I've no use for your money."

"I don't understand. Why did you do this to me, then? If you don't want the money, what the fuck do you want?"

Obviously he did not understand. It was like trying to communicate with an alien. Trying to explain to a man like Tano Raschillà that the money had to go back to the state. That it could pay for a school, perhaps. A hospital. Save a town from financial meltdown. Clean up a polluting factory. A waste of time. A waste of effort.

"I want a full and unconditional confession. And along with the confession, I want you to surrender the money. Now is it clear what I want?"

"But if you already have the money, why do I need to . . .?"

Like banging your head against a brick wall. They really were living in parallel universes! Patiently, Federico explained that his problem was justifying where the money had come from. During the night he had diverted the two billion into one of his own accounts. He certainly could not go to the Public Prosecutor and say, "Here's a bunch of money I've taken from the 'ndrangheta and the narcos. Of course I committed about thirty different crimes of varying degrees of seriousness to get my hands on it, but hey, what can you do?"

To end the game, he had to get back on the right side of the law.

"You've got no idea who's behind that money," Raschillà spluttered, finally getting the picture.

"Are you talking about Don Achille?"

"Him and others. Don Achille will have me flayed alive."

Federico glanced theatrically at the old fake Raketa watch he had bought from a street vendor at Lake Maggiore.

"Right about now, Don Achille should be in Opera Prison."

"Are you sure about that?"

"Give or take a minute . . ."

With a tortured sigh, Raschillà gave in.

Give or take a minute, Don Achille Patriarca was picked up at 4.15 p.m. while preparing to inaugurate the new *bocce* court at the "Antonino Scopelliti" social club. Before being hand-cuffed, he asked permission to make a telephone call.

"To my wife, Carmen. If I don't get home for dinner, she might worry . . ."

The Central Operations Unit officer repressed the instinct to give him a kick in the balls and snapped the handcuffs onto his wrists.

"You can call later, from the station," he said coldly.

Millions of T.V. viewers enjoyed the headline scene on the evening news.

While a subtitle explained that "a brilliant joint operation conducted by the Central Operations Unit, the Anti-Mafia Investigation Department and the Finance Police had led to the recovery of an enormous sum of money deriving from drug trafficking," images of Don Achille and his trusty hitmen being arrested were followed by a brief interview with one of the members of the social club, conducted by a Sky News24 reporter.

"Signor Brusagatti . . ."

"*Ragioniere.*"

"I beg your pardon, Ragionier Brusagatti. You're one of the leading members of this club. Tell me, did you know Achille Patriarca?"

"I certainly did!"

"And what can you tell us about him?"

"I never liked him. Don't get me wrong, he seemed nice, happy to help . . . but at the end of the day . . ."

"At the end of the day?"

"Well, what can I say? Certain looks, certain implications . . . the people who sometimes came to see him . . . I just didn't like it. You could tell there was something strange about that man . . ."

"But you never told anyone of your suspicions?"

"How could I? He was the president, they all followed him around, asking for favours . . . But I mean, if you don't know how someone earns a living, someone who came out of nowhere . . . a

southerner . . . Don't get me wrong, I'm not racist.
I've even got a few friends from Puglia . . . but
basically, I kept my distance from him."

"Thank you, Signor Brusagatti."

"*Ragioniere.*"

After waiting for an hour, Mr Collins realised that the Italian, that fucking arsehole, was not going to call back.

He had no choice but to send the official notification to Head Office.

Lord Bruegel, chairman and principal shareholder of the Intertrade Bank, was in Wales, on the fifteenth hole at his golf club, when his private secretary took a call on the mobile. Lord Bruegel came from a family of German aristocrats. They had thrown in their lot with the House of Hanover, with which he could claim a distant kinship. He was an old gentleman of impeccable manners and impossible character. And he hated to be disturbed during a game of golf. Especially in circumstances like these, when his opponent was a half-breed Indian or Pakistani. Even though the fellow was from a former colony, Bruegel still had to butter him up in the name of business. So he told Simpkins to tell the caller to go to hell, and was extremely surprised when his secretary put his foot down.

"With all due respect, My Lord, I believe you ought to come to the telephone."

Snorting like a bull, Lord Bruegel handed the caddy the

sand wedge he was holding and got Simpkins to give him the phone.

"There's a bit of a shit storm brewing, old man," croaked Lord Tremayne, head of the Financial Services Authority.

The next day, Lord Bruegel met Lord Tremayne at his office in the City.

Lord Bruegel handed him a dossier, complete with names and figures, in which he had reconstructed the affair of the "suspect" account at the Providenciales subsidiary, placing responsibility squarely on the shoulders of Collins, the director. Lord Tremayne took the fabricated dossier at face value. A doctored version of the truth would be passed to the courts and go down in history, stating that Collins had authorised the bank's acceptance of money of dubious provenance on his own initiative, ignoring specific directives from the bank's chairman, and acting without his knowledge, in open violation of instructions he had received. A vigorous handshake sufficed to conclude the conversation. Over and above their shared membership of a particular social class and a friendship dating back to their time at Oxford, a crucial aspect of their relationship was their shared allegiance to the law of money: when it's there, it doesn't smell; when it starts to stink, you sweep it under someone else's carpet.

The news of the confiscation of two billion euros took a few days to spread around the world. In the meantime, details were

fleshed out and further names emerged. When the cartel discovered that its money had gone missing, and that the Italian
banker was responsible, El Rubio, who had stood guarantee
for him, was urgently called to Guadalajara for clarification.

Reading between the lines: a death sentence.

El Rubio threw a few things into a rucksack, loaded a
machine gun and two pistols, grabbed his stash of dollars and
prepared himself for a life on the run. He planned to make for
Venezuela, where he had been keeping a safe house for some
time. From there, if the cartel didn't get him first, he would try
his luck in Europe. He had wanted for some time to visit Spain.
With a bit of luck, a smart guy like him could start again. But
in the meantime, he had to move. Right away.

He called for Felipe. He had grown fond of the boy, who,
in turn, mindful of the mercy he had been shown, had proved
himself to be obedient and loyal. Above all loyal.

Felipe was on the telephone.

"Just a second, boss!"

"You can talk to your girlfriend some other time. For fuck's
sake, Felipe, I told you to hurry up!"

El Rubio went out to the armoured Hummer. Felipe
caught up with him.

And put two bullets in the back of his neck.

Then he pocketed his gun, pushed El Rubio's body aside
and climbed into the driver's seat. As he drove to Guadalajara,

he thought about what the man from the cartel had said to him on the telephone.

"You'll take El Rubio's place. We need people like you."

Money. An end to poverty. A house for his mother. A real house, with modern furniture, satellite T.V. and a little football pitch out back. His brothers would go to school. One of them might become a doctor or an engineer, who knew. They were good kids, and he would provide for their future.

As for Uncle Jorge, he would give him a wad of pesos and an S.U.V.

The only way was up, up, up.

And coke, God bless it, was the elevator.

Patching things up with Terry proved more difficult than he had thought it might be, but in the end the journalist let herself be persuaded and got back together with Federico Anselmi. He liked her. She was down to earth but had fire in her veins. Federico began to imagine a relationship that might last longer than the usual six or seven weeks, after which boredom and anxiety inevitably took the upper hand, and he started to dream of fresh embraces, fresh scents and fresh adventures.

Terry was very fond of her new man. If only he was a little less rigid when it came to certain things . . . Then again, he was a policeman. With a degree and from a good family, and perhaps even a bit wild in his own way, but at the end of the day still a policeman.

She was lying naked on the bed, anticipating the pleasures to come as she sipped a small whisky, to a sensual soundtrack provided by Skin's unmistakable vocals.

Terry checked her makeup one last time in the mirror, then snorted a couple of lines.

Now she was ready.

MASSIMO CARLOTTO was born in Padua in 1956. In January 1976, he stumbled across a brutally murdered body in his hometown. He was accused of the murder and, just before the appeal, he went on the run. Captured finally in Mexico, he was sent back to Italy and eventually to prison. He was pardoned in 1993. It was one of the most controversial cases in Italian legal history. His first book, *Il fuggiasco*, was autobiographical, after which he began a crime series in which the main character, Alligator, is a former convict who becomes a detective. His crime novels have won many prizes both in Italy and abroad.

GIANRICO CAROFIGLIO, born in 1951, is a novelist and former anti-Mafia judge in the Italian city of Bari. His first novel, *Involuntary Witness* (Bitter Lemon Press) was published in English in 2005 and has since been adapted as the basis for a popular Italian television series. In 2005 Carofiglio was the winner of the Premio Bancarella for his novel *The Past is a Foreign Country*. He is also Honorary President of the Edinburgh Gadda Prize, which celebrates the work of Carlo Emilio Gadda.

GIANCARLO DE CATALDO was born in Taranto, Apulia, in 1956. In addition to being a novelist, essayist, translator and the author of numerous scripts and screenplays, he is also a judge in the court of Rome. His acclaimed novel *Romanzo criminale* (2002) is inspired by the true story of a powerful criminal gang active in Rome in the 1970s, known as "Banda della Maglian". He is also the editor of *Crimini*, the Bitter Lemon book of Italian crime fiction. He is currently Visiting Professor in the School of Law, Birkbeck, University of London.